Wild
and
Wanton
Edition

Daisy Miller

Gabrielle Vigot *and* Henry James

CRIMSON
ROMANCE
F+W Media, Inc.

This edition published by
Crimson Romance
an imprint of F+W Media, Inc.
10151 Carver Road, Suite 200
Blue Ash, Ohio 45242
www.crimsonromance.com

ISBN 10: 1-4405-6860-X
ISBN 13: 978-1-4405-6860-2
eISBN 10: 1-4405-6861-8
eISBN 13: 978-1-4405-6861-9

I dedicate this salacious novella to sexy mama Marti-Kini, Matt, and my lovely, supportive friends and family.

Acknowledgments

Thanks are in order to everyone who gave me guidance and a chance at Crimson Romance, particularly Jess Verdi, Jennifer Lawler, Tara Gelsomino, Julie Sturgeon, and Beth Gunn.

Foreword

Bonjour, treasured readers!

I'm author Gabrielle Vigot, and I've just completed my first project for Crimson Romance, a Wild and Wanton edition of Henry James's *Daisy Miller*. I thank you sublimely for purchasing this sexed-up novella. As you may know, Wild and Wanton editions are written based on the classic novels you cherish. But then the authors go all wild n' wanton on the original prose— and what you end up with is the story of the original characters with subplots and sexy new scenes of them doing what you always secretly wanted them to do—having wild and crazy sex with each other.

You see, in the 1800s, authors simply didn't write about their treasured characters making love under the stars, or getting hot and heavy in the castles they visited. And their petticoats most certainly didn't slip off in the hands of handsome strangers before marriage. Yet these are all things that could have happened, and are often implied, within the original story arcs.

I chose *Daisy Miller* as my Wild and Wanton story because of the sexual tension between the two main characters, Daisy and Winterbourne. Throughout the book, Winterbourne tries to rein her in and tries to convince her to behave better than a "little American flirt," but as Daisy points out numerous times, she has "never allowed a gentleman to dictate" to her, or to "interfere with anything" she does. She flirts with various gentlemen, to the outrage of the high-society vacationers she longs to join. It's a novella about the stifling social mores of the late 1800s, a wild and wanton young woman, and the man who busies himself with the delectable chore of trying to rein her in.

PART I

At the little town of Vevey, in Switzerland, there is a particularly comfortable hotel. There are, indeed, many hotels, for the entertainment of tourists is the business of the place, which, as many travelers will remember, is seated upon the edge of a remarkably blue lake—a lake that it behooves every tourist to visit. The shore of the lake presents an unbroken array of establishments of this order, of every category, from the "grand hotel" of the newest fashion, with a chalk-white front, a hundred balconies, and a dozen flags flying from its roof, to the little Swiss pension of an elder day, with its name inscribed in German-looking lettering upon a pink or yellow wall and an awkward summerhouse in the angle of the garden.

One of the hotels at Vevey, however, is famous, even classical, being distinguished from many of its upstart neighbors by an air both of luxury and of maturity. In this region, in the month of June, American travelers are extremely numerous; it may be said, indeed, that Vevey assumes at this period some of the characteristics of an American watering place. There are sights and sounds which evoke a vision, an echo, of Newport and Saratoga. There is a flitting hither and thither of "stylish" young girls, a rustling of muslin flounces, a rattle of dance music in the morning hours, a sound of high-pitched voices at all times.

You receive an impression of these things at the excellent inn of the "Trois Couronnes" and are transported in fancy to the Ocean House or to Congress Hall. But at the "Trois Couronnes," it must be added, there are other features that are much at variance with these suggestions: neat German waiters, who look like secretaries of legation; Russian princesses sitting in the garden; little Polish boys walking about held by the hand, with their governors; a view of the sunny crest of the Dent du Midi and the picturesque towers of the Castle of Chillon.

I hardly know whether it was the analogies or the differences that were uppermost in the mind of a young American, who, two or three years ago, sat in the garden of the "Trois Couronnes," looking about him, rather idly, at some of the graceful objects I have mentioned. It was a beautiful summer morning, and in whatever fashion the young American looked at things, they must have seemed to him charming. He had come from Geneva the day before by the little steamer, to see his aunt, who was staying at the hotel—Geneva having been for a long time his place of residence. But his aunt had a headache—his aunt had almost always a headache—and now she was shut up in her room, smelling camphor, so that he was at liberty to wander about. He was some seven-and-twenty years of age; when his friends spoke of him, they usually said that he was at Geneva "studying."

When his enemies spoke of him, they said—but, after all, he had no enemies; he was an extremely amiable fellow, and universally liked. What I should say is, simply, that when certain persons spoke of him they affirmed that the reason of his spending so much time at Geneva was that he was extremely devoted to a lady who lived there—a foreign lady—a person older than himself. Very few Americans—indeed, I think none—had ever seen this lady, about whom there were some singular stories. But Winterbourne had an old attachment for the little metropolis of Calvinism; he had been put to school there as a boy, and he had afterward gone to college there—circumstances which had led to his forming a great many youthful friendships. Many of these he had kept, and they were a source of great satisfaction to him.

After knocking at his aunt's door and learning that she was indisposed, he had taken a walk about the town, and then he had come in to his breakfast. He had now finished his breakfast; but he was drinking a small cup of coffee, which had been served to him on a little table in the garden by one of the waiters who looked like an attaché . At last he finished his coffee and lit a cigarette. Presently a small boy came walking along the path— an urchin of nine or ten. The child, who was diminutive for his years, had an aged expression of countenance, a pale complexion, and sharp little features. He was dressed in knickerbockers, with red stockings, which displayed his poor little spindle-shanks; he also wore a brilliant red cravat. He carried in his hand a long alpenstock, the sharp point of which he thrust into everything that he approached—the flowerbeds, the garden benches, the trains of the ladies' dresses. In front of Winterbourne he paused, looking at him with a pair of bright, penetrating little eyes.

"Will you give me a lump of sugar?" he asked in a sharp, hard little voice—a voice immature and yet, somehow, not young.

Winterbourne glanced at the small table near him, on which his coffee service rested, and saw that several morsels of sugar remained. "Yes, you may take one," he answered; "but I don't think sugar is good for little boys."

This little boy stepped forward and carefully selected three of the coveted fragments, two of which he buried in the pocket of his knickerbockers, depositing the other as promptly in another place. He poked his alpenstock, lance-fashion, into Winterbourne's bench and tried to crack the lump of sugar with his teeth.

"Oh, blazes; it's har-r-d!" he exclaimed, pronouncing the adjective in a peculiar manner.

Winterbourne had immediately perceived that he might have the honor of claiming him as a fellow countryman. "Take care you don't hurt your teeth," he said, paternally.

"I haven't got any teeth to hurt. They have all come out. I have only got seven teeth. My mother counted them last night, and one came out right afterward. She said she'd slap me if any more came out. I can't help it. It's this old Europe. It's the climate that makes them come out. In America they didn't come out. It's these hotels."

Winterbourne was much amused. "If you eat three lumps of sugar, your mother will certainly slap you," he said.

"She's got to give me some candy, then," rejoined his young interlocutor. "I can't get any candy here—any American candy. American candy's the best candy."

"And are American little boys the best little boys?" asked Winterbourne.

"I don't know. I'm an American boy," said the child.

"I see you are one of the best!" laughed Winterbourne.

"Are you an American man?" pursued this vivacious infant. And then, on Winterbourne's affirmative reply—"American men are the best," he declared.

His companion thanked him for the compliment, and the child, who had now got astride of his alpenstock, stood looking about him, while he attacked a second lump of sugar. Winterbourne wondered if he himself had been like this in his infancy, for he had been brought to Europe at about this age.

"Here comes my sister!" cried the child in a moment. "She's an American girl."

Winterbourne looked along the path and saw a beautiful young lady advancing. "American girls are the best girls," he said cheerfully to his young companion.

"My sister ain't the best!" the child declared. "She's always blowing at me."

"I imagine that is your fault, not hers," said Winterbourne. The young lady meanwhile had drawn near. She was dressed in white muslin, with a hundred frills and flounces, and knots of pale-colored ribbon. She was bareheaded, but she balanced in her hand a large parasol, with a deep border of embroidery; and she was strikingly, admirably pretty. "How pretty they are!" thought Winterbourne, straightening himself in his seat, as if he were prepared to rise.

The young lady paused in front of his bench, near the parapet of the garden, which overlooked the lake. The little boy had now converted his alpenstock into a vaulting pole, by the aid of which he was springing about in the gravel and kicking it up not a little.

"Randolph," said the young lady, "what *are* you doing?"

"I'm going up the Alps," replied Randolph. "This is the way!" And he gave another little jump, scattering the pebbles about Winterbourne's ears.

"That's the way they come down," said Winterbourne.

"He's an American man!" cried Randolph, in his little hard voice.

The young lady gave no heed to this announcement, but looked straight at her brother. "Well, I guess you had better be quiet," she simply observed.

It seemed to Winterbourne that he had been in a manner presented. He got up and stepped slowly toward the young girl, throwing away his cigarette. "This little boy and I have made acquaintance," he said, with great civility. In Geneva, as he had been perfectly aware, a young man was not at liberty to speak to a young unmarried lady except under certain rarely occurring conditions; but here at Vevey, what conditions could be better than these?—a pretty American girl coming and standing in front of you in a garden. This pretty American girl, however, on hearing Winterbourne's observation, simply glanced at him; she then turned her head and looked over the parapet, at the lake and the opposite mountains. The garden's red and white roses were quite alike to the lakeside varietals with their intoxicating perfumes, and he noticed the scent wafting from the girl was dissimilar, but invited his curiosity all the more.

He wasn't a stray hound!—he admonished himself. But as he was at his best a civilized young man, Winterbourne allowed himself simple pleasures and thus immediately let his thoughts wander. Firstly, what would he imagine lay beneath those flounces and folds of her country dress?

He mustn't let himself go that far. She was the picture of youth. Yet just as her now darker, now vulnerable eyes steadily locked with his for the first time, he saw a flicker of what she would look like in her private bath, in whichever one of the European hotels her mother might have taken her on vacation. The girl would have disrobed quietly, for him achingly:

The dying soap sheen on her naked back, a smirk as she let her hair down, her hungering body unaware that she was but a figment. Her small, upward breasts with the rivulets from her bathing sponge pulsing in her shiver from the open window.

Her heart beating as she favored her inner thigh with her fingers, as lush and heartbreaking as last evening's fuchsia peonies back in the reality of their current hotel—but he must have stopped himself a dozen times from fancies such as those in the minutes he gazed about the view with her.

He then dared a glance, and upon meeting her questioning eyes after she kept Randolph from his alpenstock yet again, he continued to hold her in his reverie and discarded a few minutes as he peered into the lake. She wasn't interested much in chatter, he supposed, as she was turning away often.

And yes, again there was her age. A nineteen-year-old American! And upon chatting, like the others, she might well be too garrulous for her own good. Yet—probably closer to Randolph's maturity than his own, there was no harm in letting her linger in his imagination. These thoughts were more to his liking than made him comfortable in polite daydreaming:

Her now sweet eyes above the flushed and excitable neck, goose pimples on their waiting arms, her lips would draw his eyes to them just as the perspiring lake would. She'd slither under the water with the pale shapes of her body elongated, he would watch her and her nakedness would draw no blush from *him*.

She'd stand back at this other hotel, perhaps in Italy, naked at the bureau. Her even complexion would show itself completely and finally, her sex peeking from behind her hands as she covered it, shyly, and between fine legs, tanned gradually from midsummer days of skirt-hiking with the other American girls when they thought they were alone. Her curled lips again, parting in a now mischievous grin—she would make for a singular soubrette!—making him want to roughly clench her bottom in his awkward hands and squeeze her engorging sex until she cried out. He wanted more than that: He wanted to claim her little body on his own and press upon it and make his way into it, thrusting himself upon and into her until she half-fainted with pleasure, until her intentions to deny him changed and her desire gave into the hot, petulant shoving of his prick under the soft hairs of her pubis, into her waiting quim.

But of course, he wouldn't daydream and torture himself more, being that he was in a game of cat and mouse with his own lovely meditations. He was smiling like a loon, and abruptly excused himself to walk around the corner and wipe it off. Winterbourne returned to the girl, stepping lightly.

He wondered whether he had gone too far, but he decided that he must advance farther, rather than retreat. While he was thinking of something else to say, the young lady turned to the little boy again.

"I should like to know where you got that pole," she said.

"I bought it," responded Randolph.

"You don't mean to say you're going to take it to Italy?"

"Yes, I am going to take it to Italy," the child declared.

The young girl glanced over the front of her dress and smoothed out a knot or two of ribbon. Then she rested her eyes upon the prospect again. "Well, I guess you had better leave it somewhere," she said after a moment.

"Are you going to Italy?" Winterbourne inquired in a tone of great respect.

The young lady glanced at him again. "Yes, sir," she replied. And she said nothing more.

"Are you—a—going over the Simplon?" Winterbourne pursued, a little embarrassed.

"I don't know," she said. "I suppose it's some mountain. Randolph, what mountain are we going over?"

"Going where?" the child demanded.

"To Italy," Winterbourne explained.

"I don't know," said Randolph. "I don't want to go to Italy. I want to go to America."

"Oh, Italy is a beautiful place!" rejoined the young man.

"Can you get candy there?" Randolph loudly inquired.

"I hope not," said his sister. "I guess you have had enough candy, and mother thinks so too."

"I haven't had any for ever so long—for a hundred weeks!" cried the boy, still jumping about.

The young lady inspected her flounces and smoothed her ribbons again; and Winterbourne presently risked an observation upon the beauty of the view. He was ceasing to be embarrassed, for he had begun to perceive that she was not in the least embarrassed herself. There had not been the slightest alteration in her charming complexion; she was evidently neither offended nor flattered. If she looked another way when he spoke to her, and seemed not particularly to hear him, this was simply her habit, her manner. Yet, as he talked a little more and pointed out some of the objects of interest in the view, with which she appeared quite unacquainted, she gradually gave him more of the benefit of her glance; and then he saw that this glance was perfectly direct and unshrinking. It was not, however, what would have been called an immodest glance, for the young girl's eyes were singularly honest and fresh. They were wonderfully pretty eyes; and, indeed, Winterbourne had not seen for a long time anything prettier than his fair countrywoman's various features—her complexion, her nose, her ears, her teeth.

He had a great relish for feminine beauty; he was addicted to observing and analyzing it; and as regards this young lady's face he made several observations. It was not at all insipid, but it was not exactly expressive; and though it was eminently delicate, Winterbourne mentally accused it—very forgivingly—of a want of finish. He thought it very possible that Master Randolph's sister was a coquette; he was sure she had a spirit of her own; but in her bright, sweet, superficial little visage there was no mockery, no irony. Before long it became obvious that she was much disposed toward conversation.

She told him that they were going to Rome for the winter—she and her mother and Randolph. She asked him if he was a "real American"; she shouldn't have taken him for one; he seemed more like a German—this was said after a little hesitation—especially when he spoke. Winterbourne, laughing, answered that he had met Germans who spoke like Americans, but that he had not, so far as he remembered, met an American who spoke like a German. Then he asked her if she should not be more comfortable in sitting upon the bench which he had just quitted. She answered that she liked standing up and walking about; but she presently sat down. She told him she was from New York State—"if you know where that is." Winterbourne learned more about her by catching hold of her small, slippery brother and making him stand a few minutes by his side.

"Tell me your name, my boy," he said.

"Randolph C. Miller," said the boy sharply. "And I'll tell you her name;" and he leveled his alpenstock at his sister.

"You had better wait till you are asked!" said this young lady calmly.

"I should like very much to know your name," said Winterbourne.

"Her name is Daisy Miller!" cried the child. "But that isn't her real name; that isn't her name on her cards."

"It's a pity you haven't got one of my cards!" said Miss Miller.

"Her real name is Annie P. Miller," the boy went on.

"Ask him HIS name," said his sister, indicating Winterbourne.

But on this point Randolph seemed perfectly indifferent; he continued to supply information with regard to his own family. "My father's name is Ezra B. Miller," he announced. "My father ain't in Europe; my father's in a better place than Europe."

Winterbourne imagined for a moment that this was the manner in which the child had been taught to intimate that Mr. Miller had been removed to the sphere of celestial reward. But Randolph immediately added, "My father's in Schenectady. He's got a big business. My father's rich, you bet!"

"Well!" ejaculated Miss Miller, lowering her parasol and looking at the embroidered border. Winterbourne presently released the child, who departed, dragging his alpenstock along the path. "He doesn't like Europe," said the young girl. "He wants to go back."

"To Schenectady, you mean?"

"Yes; he wants to go right home. He hasn't got any boys here. There is one boy here, but he always goes round with a teacher; they won't let him play."

"And your brother hasn't any teacher?" Winterbourne inquired.

"Mother thought of getting him one, to travel round with us. There was a lady told her of a very good teacher; an American lady—perhaps you know her—Mrs. Sanders. I think she came from Boston. She told her of this teacher, and we thought of getting him to travel round with us. But Randolph said he didn't want a teacher traveling round with us. He said he wouldn't have lessons when he was in the cars. And we ARE in the cars about half the time. There was an English lady we met in the cars—I think her name was Miss Featherstone; perhaps you know her. She wanted to know why I didn't give Randolph lessons—give him 'instruction,' she called it. I guess he could give me more instruction than I could give him. He's very smart."

"Yes," said Winterbourne; "he seems very smart."

"Mother's going to get a teacher for him as soon as we get to Italy. Can you get good teachers in Italy?"

"Very good, I should think," said Winterbourne.

"Or else she's going to find some school. He ought to learn some more. He's only nine. He's going to college." And in this way Miss Miller continued to converse upon the affairs of her family and upon other topics. She sat there with her extremely pretty hands, ornamented with very brilliant rings, folded in her lap, and with her pretty eyes now resting upon those of Winterbourne, now wandering over the garden, the people who passed by, and the beautiful view. She talked to Winterbourne as if she had known him a long time. He found it very pleasant. It was many years since he had heard a young girl talk so much.

It might have been said of this unknown young lady, who had come and sat down beside him upon a bench, that she chattered. She was very quiet; she sat in a charming, tranquil attitude; but her lips and her eyes were constantly moving. She had a soft, slender, agreeable voice, and her tone was decidedly sociable. She gave Winterbourne a history of her movements and intentions and those of her mother and brother, in Europe, and enumerated, in particular, the various hotels at which they had stopped. "That English lady in the cars," she said—"Miss Featherstone—asked me if we didn't all live in hotels in America. I told her I had never been in so many hotels in my life as since I came to Europe. I have never seen so many—it's nothing but hotels." But Miss Miller did not make this remark with a querulous accent; she appeared to be in the best humor with everything. She declared that the hotels were very good, when once you got used to their ways, and that Europe was perfectly sweet. She was not disappointed—not a bit. Perhaps it was because she had heard so much about it before. She had ever so many intimate friends that had been there ever so many times. And then she had had ever so many dresses and things from Paris. Whenever she put on a Paris dress she felt as if she were in Europe.

"It was a kind of a wishing cap," said Winterbourne.

"Yes," said Miss Miller without examining this analogy; "it always made me wish I was here. But I needn't have done that for dresses. I am sure they send all the pretty ones to America; you see the most frightful things here. The only thing I don't like," she proceeded, "is the society. There isn't any society; or, if there is, I don't know where it keeps itself. Do you? I suppose there is some society somewhere, but I haven't seen anything of it. I'm very fond of society, and I have always had a great deal of it. I don't mean only in Schenectady, but in New York. I used to go to New York every winter. In New York I had lots of society. Last winter I had seventeen dinners given me; and three of them were by gentlemen," added Daisy Miller. "I have more friends in New York than in Schenectady—more gentleman friends; and more young lady friends too," she resumed in a moment.

She paused again for an instant; she was looking at Winterbourne with all her prettiness in her lively eyes and in her light, slightly monotonous smile. "I have always had," she said, "a great deal of gentlemen's society." Daisy smiled to herself as she recalled a few of these *gentleman friends*. Though she was conscious of hoping for Winterbourne's eventual friendship and sensed he might be a better man, and more gentle, than the rough ones she knew from New York, she found it hard to keep her imagination under control. She felt heat pulse through her, coming from between her legs for several seconds, and somehow managed to excuse herself to walk round the corner. She was sweating in the summer sunshine and was suddenly very uncomfortable in her three-tiered skirt and silk stockings.

She had wanted to stop on the trip to Vevey at the Plage de Curtineaux at night, alone, and search for *other* friends. She'd wanted to feel intoxicated, as she did back home, in the presence of foreign men. What she would have given to finally fulfill her sense of longing, to give in to pleasures only married women could admit to! In the frigid months of the Schenectady winter, she had desired to lower her own frigidity in the company of gentlemen. She'd become anxious in a way that had plagued her since pubescence. It was a sweet anxiety, and one that made her pulse in anticipation. She had, many times, thanked the gods that it was invisible to the outside world, but it encouraged her to go on the qui vive for male company, if only to sit in their presence and laugh awhile together. She had had her share of dalliances, but never before had she allowed a man such liberties as she did a fortnight ago in her cousin's home upstate.

Away from the kind, warm eyes of Winterbourne and other prying hotel guests, she allowed herself to remember, the sweet feeling emanating from her sex as she stole behind the parapet and thought of that night. She rubbed her skirts over her thin thighs, more and more directly on and under her feminine mound as her pleasure grew.

During her cousin Daphne's annual masquerade, the mid-winter soirée, Daisy had felt out of sorts, and thought perhaps her cousin's fiendishly handsome friend Isaac could ease her discomfort. She shivered recalling his tall frame, the way he ran his hands through his wavy brown hair, and his broad and rough, yet exquisitely knowledgeable, hands on her. Daphne had whispered about Isaac at the party, and how, though he was ever discreet and feigned innocence when questioned, he had "ways with women" that made him quite the eligible bachelor. He had been casual at the party, looking Daisy's way and smiling at her several times until she bent over the table of canapés, whereupon he had made his way across the party to her, staring rudely at her décolletage and almost tripping over himself on the way over. She'd meant to *slap* him, but instead followed him into the kitchen on the pretense of gathering Daphne's silver for another guest. Isaac having taken Daisy's hand, the pair had snuck out of the back door. After he had bestowed upon her a flurry of slavish compliments, she had told Isaac that he was mildly attractive, and he shut up and she looked down and noticed his massive erection.

Without so much as a tiny kiss, he smiled at her in a most naughty way.

His skillful hands had forcefully pushed up her skirts and then pulled down her bodice. He rubbed her mound while alternating between her nipples, sucking fiercely and causing her exquisite torture. When his index finger slipped into her wet slit, she almost screamed in pleasure.

He put up his hand to her mouth and told her she mustn't make a sound or he would stop. And then she wouldn't be having so much fun, would she? Daisy had breathlessly sworn to keep quiet in the empty night. He had cupped a damp hand over her mouth and carefully tried to slither a second finger into her while pulling her taut nipple roughly into his mouth with his teeth.

As she felt her climax rise, he swiftly pulled his fingers out of her and started moving his head away from her breasts. Distraught over the sudden loss of gratification, Daisy cried out in anguish. Isaac meant to continue to play with her body until he burst his hot fluid on her, and she knew this. He slanted his tongue over her hottest spot, her flowering, engorged bud, and began to suck at her, lapping greedily at her juices. This pushed Daisy over the edge, and she bit her tongue hard to keep from screaming out from between his fingers, still over her mouth. She gave Isaac a reward for his efforts, a small shudder, and she knew she was the closest to ecstasy she'd ever been.

After Daisy's fantasy faded, she pulled down her skirts and took to wondering whether Winterbourne might have been as skilled would he have been given the chance to touch her in the fresh snow as Isaac had. Daisy quietly stepped over to Winterbourne and announced her return to him with a winning smile.

Poor Winterbourne was amused, perplexed, and decidedly charmed. He had never yet heard a young girl express herself in just this fashion; never, at least, save in cases where to say such things seemed a kind of demonstrative evidence of a certain laxity of deportment. And yet was he to accuse Miss Daisy Miller of actual or potential *inconduite*, as they said at Geneva? He felt that he had lived at Geneva so long that he had lost a good deal; he had become dishabituated to the American tone. Never, indeed, since he had grown old enough to appreciate things, had he encountered a young American girl of so pronounced a type as this. Certainly she was very charming, but how deucedly sociable! Was she simply a pretty girl from New York State? Were they all like that, the pretty girls who had a good deal of gentlemen's society? Or was she also a designing, an audacious, an unscrupulous young person?

Winterbourne had lost his instinct in this matter, and his reason could not help him. Miss Daisy Miller looked extremely innocent. Some people had told him that, after all, American girls were exceedingly innocent; and others had told him that, after all, they were not. He was inclined to think Miss Daisy Miller was a flirt—a pretty American flirt. He had never, as yet, had any relations with young ladies of this category. He had known, here in Europe, two or three women—persons older than Miss Daisy Miller, and provided, for respectability's sake, with husbands—who were great coquettes—dangerous, terrible women, with whom one's relations were liable to take a serious turn. But this young girl was not a coquette in that sense; she was very unsophisticated; she was only a pretty American flirt.

Winterbourne was almost grateful for having found the formula that applied to Miss Daisy Miller. He leaned back in his seat; he remarked to himself that she had the most charming nose he had ever seen; he wondered what were the regular conditions and limitations of one's intercourse with a pretty American flirt. It presently became apparent that he was on the way to learn.

"Have you been to that old castle?" asked the young girl, pointing with her parasol to the far-gleaming walls of the Chateau de Chillon.

"Yes, formerly, more than once," said Winterbourne. "You too, I suppose, have seen it?"

"No; we haven't been there. I want to go there dreadfully. Of course I mean to go there. I wouldn't go away from here without having seen that old castle."

"It's a very pretty excursion," said Winterbourne, "and very easy to make. You can drive, you know, or you can go by the little steamer."

"You can go in the cars," said Miss Miller.

"Yes; you can go in the cars," Winterbourne assented.

"Our courier says they take you right up to the castle," the young girl continued. "We were going last week, but my mother gave out. She suffers dreadfully from dyspepsia. She said she couldn't go. Randolph wouldn't go either; he says he doesn't think much of old castles. But I guess we'll go this week, if we can get Randolph."

"Your brother is not interested in ancient monuments?" Winterbourne inquired, smiling.

"He says he don't care much about old castles. He's only nine. He wants to stay at the hotel. Mother's afraid to leave him alone, and the courier won't stay with him; so we haven't been to many places. But it will be too bad if we don't go up there." And Miss Miller pointed again at the Chateau de Chillon.

"I should think it might be arranged," said Winterbourne. "Couldn't you get some one to stay for the afternoon with Randolph?"

Miss Miller looked at him a moment, and then, very placidly, "I wish *you* would stay with him!" she said.

Winterbourne hesitated a moment. "I should much rather go to Chillon with you."

"With me?" asked the young girl with the same placidity.

She didn't rise, blushing, as a young girl at Geneva would have done; and yet Winterbourne, conscious that he had been very bold, thought it possible she was offended. "With your mother," he answered very respectfully.

But it seemed that both his audacity and his respect were lost upon Miss Daisy Miller. "I guess my mother won't go, after all," she said. "She doesn't like to ride round in the afternoon. But did you really mean what you said just now—that you would like to go up there?"

"Most earnestly," Winterbourne declared.

"Then we may arrange it. If mother will stay with Randolph, I guess Eugenio will."

"Eugenio?" the young man inquired.

"Eugenio's our courier. He doesn't like to stay with Randolph; he's the most fastidious man I ever saw. But he's a splendid courier. I guess he'll stay at home with Randolph if mother does, and then we can go to the castle."

Winterbourne reflected for an instant as lucidly as possible—"we" could only mean Miss Daisy Miller and himself. This program seemed almost too agreeable for credence; he felt as if he ought to kiss the young lady's hand. Possibly he would have done so and quite spoiled the project, but at this moment another person, presumably Eugenio, appeared. A tall, handsome man, with superb whiskers, wearing a velvet morning coat and a brilliant watch chain, approached Miss Miller, looking sharply at her companion. "Oh, Eugenio!" said Miss Miller with the friendliest accent.

Eugenio had looked at Winterbourne from head to foot; he now bowed gravely to the young lady. "I have the honor to inform mademoiselle that luncheon is upon the table."

Miss Miller slowly rose. "See here, Eugenio!" she said; "I'm going to that old castle, anyway."

"To the Chateau de Chillon, mademoiselle?" the courier inquired. "Mademoiselle has made arrangements?" he added in a tone which struck Winterbourne as very impertinent.

Eugenio's tone apparently threw, even to Miss Miller's own apprehension, a slightly ironical light upon the young girl's situation. She turned to Winterbourne, blushing a little—a very little. "You won't back out?" she said.

"I shall not be happy till we go!" he protested.

"And you are staying in this hotel?" she went on. "And you are really an American?"

The courier stood looking at Winterbourne offensively. The young man, at least, thought his manner of looking an offense to Miss Miller; it conveyed an imputation that she "picked up" acquaintances. "I shall have the honor of presenting to you a person who will tell you all about me," he said, smiling and referring to his aunt.

"Oh, well, we'll go some day," said Miss Miller. And she gave him a smile and turned away. She put up her parasol and walked back to the inn beside Eugenio. Winterbourne stood looking after her; and as she moved away, drawing her muslin furbelows over the gravel, said to himself that she had the tournure of a princess.

He had, however, engaged to do more than proved feasible, in promising to present his aunt, Mrs. Costello, to Miss Daisy Miller. As soon as the former lady had got better of her headache, he waited upon her in her apartment; and, after the proper inquiries in regard to her health, he asked her if she had observed in the hotel an American family—a mamma, a daughter, and a little boy.

"And a courier?" said Mrs. Costello. "Oh yes, I have observed them. Seen them—heard them—and kept out of their way." Mrs. Costello was a widow with a fortune; a person of much distinction, who frequently intimated that, if she were not so dreadfully liable to sick headaches, she would probably have left a deeper impress upon her time. She had a long, pale face, a high nose, and a great deal of very striking white hair, which she wore in large puffs and rouleaux over the top of her head. She had two sons married in New York and another who was now in Europe.

This young man was amusing himself at Hamburg, and, though he was on his travels, was rarely perceived to visit any particular city at the moment selected by his mother for her own appearance there. Her nephew, who had come up to Vevey expressly to see her, was therefore more attentive than those who, as she said, were nearer to her. He had imbibed at Geneva the idea that one must always be attentive to one's aunt. Mrs. Costello had not seen him for many years, and she was greatly pleased with him, manifesting her approbation by initiating him into many of the secrets of that social sway which, as she gave him to understand, she exerted in the American capital. She admitted that she was very exclusive; but, if he were acquainted with New York, he would see that one had to be. And her picture of the minutely hierarchical constitution of the society of that city, which she presented to him in many different lights, was, to Winterbourne's imagination, almost oppressively striking.

He immediately perceived, from her tone, that Miss Daisy Miller's place in the social scale was low. "I am afraid you don't approve of them," he said.

"They are very common," Mrs. Costello declared. "They are the sort of Americans that one does one's duty by not—not accepting."

"Ah, you don't accept them?" said the young man.

"I can't, my dear Frederick. I would if I could, but I can't."

"The young girl is very pretty," said Winterbourne in a moment.

"Of course she's pretty. But she is very common."

"I see what you mean, of course," said Winterbourne after another pause.

"She has that charming look that they all have," his aunt resumed. "I can't think where they pick it up; and she dresses in perfection—no, you don't know how well she dresses. I can't think where they get their taste."

"But, my dear aunt, she is not, after all, a Comanche savage."

"She is a young lady," said Mrs. Costello, "who has an intimacy with her mamma's courier."

"An intimacy with the courier?" the young man demanded.

"Oh, the mother is just as bad! They treat the courier like a familiar friend—like a gentleman. I shouldn't wonder if he dines with them. Very likely they have never seen a man with such good manners, such fine clothes, so like a gentleman. He probably corresponds to the young lady's idea of a count. He sits with them in the garden in the evening. I think he smokes."

Winterbourne listened with interest to these disclosures; they helped him to make up his mind about Miss Daisy. Evidently she was rather wild. "Well," he said, "I am not a courier, and yet she was very charming to me."

"You had better have said at first," said Mrs. Costello with dignity, "that you had made her acquaintance."

"We simply met in the garden, and we talked a bit."

"Tout bonnement! And pray what did you say?"

"I said I should take the liberty of introducing her to my admirable aunt."

"I am much obliged to you."

"It was to guarantee my respectability," said Winterbourne.

"And pray who is to guarantee hers?"

"Ah, you are cruel!" said the young man. "She's a very nice young girl."

"You don't say that as if you believed it," Mrs. Costello observed.

"She is completely uncultivated," Winterbourne went on. "But she is wonderfully pretty, and, in short, she is very nice. To prove that I believe it, I am going to take her to the Chateau de Chillon."

"You two are going off there together? I should say it proved just the contrary. How long had you known her, may I ask, when this interesting project was formed? You haven't been twenty-four hours in the house."

"I have known her half an hour!" said Winterbourne, smiling.

"Dear me!" cried Mrs. Costello. "What a dreadful girl!"

Her nephew was silent for some moments. "You really think, then," he began earnestly, and with a desire for trustworthy information—"you really think that—" But he paused again.

"Think what, sir?" said his aunt.

"That she is the sort of young lady who expects a man, sooner or later, to carry her off?"

"I haven't the least idea what such young ladies expect a man to do. But I really think that you had better not meddle with little American girls that are uncultivated, as you call them. You have lived too long out of the country. You will be sure to make some great mistake. You are too innocent."

"My dear aunt, I am not so innocent," said Winterbourne, smiling and curling his mustache.

Winterbourne remonstrated himself for this small but damning admission. He remembered the blustering, ruddy women at the billiard halls during his grade school years. Frederick, Fred, as a gawking teenager, had often been offered more than his fair share of pleasure by these doxies in whispered terms. Their vacant, painted smiles had, for the most part, little effect on him, and he never took advantage of their whisperings of entente cordiale. Winterbourne had, with his young American pals, professed to save himself for love, as was the custom in high society in his boyhood.

That threw limits on his observations of the billiard women, as his more vulgar friends called them. Young Fred had noticed a few of them around the hustlers one night, but once again paid them no mind—until one of them spoke. He whipped around, having lost his concentration and expecting trickery from a friend. "Excuse m—!," he began to say, before abruptly stammering out an apology. A particularly fair-skinned girl called Rebecca, dressed with exceptional taste, held a handsome billiard stick of dark wood. Her sad almandine eyes held him for the moment, until she spoke. "I was assigned to this table by the man at the door for this night's tournament. There is no grand prize, but won't you let a lady on your team?"

Winterbourne, having regained his teen-age composure, ejected, "But we would be so honored! Is that your stick? It is—very fine." Though accustomed to few women players in the hall, and fewer allowed maces like the men, Winterbourne regarded her as a worthy challenger. She promptly won the game, which plunged him into a slightly dangerous habit of appreciating spunky, often difficult women.

An unlikely friendship formed and proceeded with caution, until one night, after Winterbourne lost what his mother would later call a nasty amount of under-the-table money to Rebecca. He had felt utterly stripped of his power as a young man. But somehow after this game, walking Rebecca home, he felt a burning desire for a woman such as this, who cared little for rules determined by her sex.

They had crossed the avenue and had just cleared the lamplight on the other side, when Rebecca turned to him as he blinked, and kissed him deeply. The unexpected closeness of her breath on his lips made him hot with a fire he hadn't experienced thusly, and he pulled her into a tight embrace. They had walked quickly into the bushes to the side, Winterbourne leading her by hand. Rebecca had told him she knew he was a raffish man at heart, and he had turned her around smoothly, pushing his hands into her waist and massaging into her soft flesh, until his hands found her pubic bone and slid below it, her dress still on.

He heard her heaving breath and laughed, the heat of the spring around them, and the bloom of the night covering them in softness. She returned the laugh, and he let his hands wander until they found her soft, supple breasts beneath her shawl. Having had too much wine for both of their sakes, he let his tongue glide over her hardening nipples, one hand cupping her pubis roughly.

He could feel her abdomen tighten under him as he moved on top of her, and he rubbed his body over her in such a way as to rub his bulging trousers over her fine skirts, which prompted her to call him a rotten scoundrel. Rebecca had grasped the bulging mass lodged in his pant leg, stroking it until neither of them dared say a word.

Then matter-of-factly, she pulled his prick out of his pants and started rubbing her petite frame over it, grinding her hips into his until she felt an orgasm creeping up on her and taking them both hostage for a few happy seconds. Little did Winterbourne's aunt know that any of this happened, as Rebecca and Winterbourne spoke little after that night, and she pursued and wed an unfortunately stuffy accountant from Brussels.

Pulled back into the current conversation with his aunt, Winterbourne attempted to give her a polite smile. Mrs. Costello paled.

"You are guilty too, then!"

Winterbourne continued to curl his mustache meditatively. "You won't let the poor girl know you then?" he asked at last.

"Is it literally true that she is going to the Chateau de Chillon with you?"

"I think that she fully intends it."

"Then, my dear Frederick," said Mrs. Costello, "I must decline the honor of her acquaintance. I am an old woman, but I am not too old, thank Heaven, to be shocked!"

"But don't they all do these things—the young girls in America?" Winterbourne inquired.

Mrs. Costello stared a moment. "I should like to see my granddaughters do them!" she declared grimly.

This seemed to throw some light upon the matter, for Winterbourne remembered to have heard that his pretty cousins in New York were "tremendous flirts." If, therefore, Miss Daisy Miller exceeded the liberal margin allowed to these young ladies, it was probable that anything might be expected of her. Winterbourne was impatient to see her again, and he was vexed with himself that, by instinct, he should not appreciate her justly.

Though he was impatient to see her, he hardly knew what he should say to her about his aunt's refusal to become acquainted with her; but he discovered, promptly enough, that with Miss Daisy Miller there was no great need of walking on tiptoe. He found her that evening in the garden, wandering about in the warm starlight like an indolent sylph, and swinging to and fro the largest fan he had ever beheld. It was ten o'clock. He had dined with his aunt, had been sitting with her since dinner, and had just taken leave of her till the morrow. Miss Daisy Miller seemed very glad to see him; she declared it was the longest evening she had ever passed.

"Have you been all alone?" he asked.

"I have been walking round with mother. But mother gets tired walking round," she answered.

"Has she gone to bed?"

"No; she doesn't like to go to bed," said the young girl. "She doesn't sleep—not three hours. She says she doesn't know how she lives. She's dreadfully nervous. I guess she sleeps more than she thinks. She's gone somewhere after Randolph; she wants to try to get him to go to bed. He doesn't like to go to bed."

"Let us hope she will persuade him," observed Winterbourne.

"She will talk to him all she can; but he doesn't like her to talk to him," said Miss Daisy, opening her fan. "She's going to try to get Eugenio to talk to him. But he isn't afraid of Eugenio. Eugenio's a splendid courier, but he can't make much impression on Randolph! I don't believe he'll go to bed before eleven." It appeared that Randolph's vigil was in fact triumphantly prolonged, for Winterbourne strolled about with the young girl for some time without meeting her mother. "I have been looking round for that lady you want to introduce me to," his companion resumed. "She's your aunt." Then, on Winterbourne's admitting the fact and expressing some curiosity as to how she had learned it, she said she had heard all about Mrs. Costello from the chambermaid.

She was very quiet and very comme il faut; she wore white puffs; she spoke to no one, and she never dined at the table d'hote. Every two days she had a headache. "I think that's a lovely description, headache and all!" said Miss Daisy, chattering along in her thin, gay voice. "I want to know her ever so much. I know just what *your* aunt would be; I know I should like her. She would be very exclusive. I like a lady to be exclusive; I'm dying to be exclusive myself. Well, we *are* exclusive, mother and I. We don't speak to everyone—or they don't speak to us. I suppose it's about the same thing. Anyway, I shall be ever so glad to know your aunt."

Winterbourne was embarrassed. "She would be most happy," he said; "but I am afraid those headaches will interfere."

The young girl looked at him through the dusk. "But I suppose she doesn't have a headache every day," she said sympathetically.

Winterbourne was silent a moment. "She tells me she does," he answered at last, not knowing what to say.

Miss Daisy Miller stopped and stood looking at him. Her prettiness was still visible in the darkness; she was opening and closing her enormous fan. "She doesn't want to know me!" she said suddenly. "Why don't you say so? You needn't be afraid. I'm not afraid!" And she gave a little laugh.

Winterbourne fancied there was a tremor in her voice; he was touched, shocked, mortified by it. "My dear young lady," he protested, "she knows no one. It's her wretched health."

The young girl walked on a few steps, laughing still. "You needn't be afraid," she repeated. "Why should she want to know me?" Then she paused again; she was close to the parapet of the garden, and in front of her was the starlit lake. There was a vague sheen upon its surface, and in the distance were dimly seen mountain forms. Daisy Miller looked out upon the mysterious prospect and then she gave another little laugh. "Gracious! she *is* exclusive!" she said. Winterbourne wondered whether she was seriously wounded, and for a moment almost wished that her sense of injury might be such as to make it becoming in him to attempt to reassure and comfort her. He had a pleasant sense that she would be very approachable for consolatory purposes.

He felt then, for the instant, quite ready to sacrifice his aunt, conversationally; to admit that she was a proud, rude woman, and to declare that they needn't mind her. But before he had time to commit himself to this perilous mixture of gallantry and impiety, the young lady, resuming her walk, gave an exclamation in quite another tone. "Well, here's Mother! I guess she hasn't got Randolph to go to bed." The figure of a lady appeared at a distance, very indistinct in the darkness, and advancing with a slow and wavering movement. Suddenly it seemed to pause.

"Are you sure it is your mother? Can you distinguish her in this thick dusk?" Winterbourne asked.

"Well!" cried Miss Daisy Miller with a laugh; "I guess I know my own mother. And when she has got on my shawl, too! She is always wearing my things."

The lady in question, ceasing to advance, hovered vaguely about the spot at which she had checked her steps.

"I am afraid your mother doesn't see you," said Winterbourne. "Or perhaps," he added, thinking, with Miss Miller, the joke permissible—"perhaps she feels guilty about your shawl."

"Oh, it's a fearful old thing!" the young girl replied serenely. "I told her she could wear it. She won't come here because she sees you."

"Ah, then," said Winterbourne, "I had better leave you."

"Oh, no; come on!" urged Miss Daisy Miller.

"I'm afraid your mother doesn't approve of my walking with you."

Miss Miller gave him a serious glance. "It isn't for me; it's for you—that is, it's for *her*. Well, I don't know who it's for! But mother doesn't like any of my gentlemen friends. She's right down timid. She always makes a fuss if I introduce a gentleman. But I *do* introduce them—almost always. If I didn't introduce my gentlemen friends to Mother," the young girl added in her little soft, flat monotone, "I shouldn't think I was natural."

"To introduce me," said Winterbourne, "you must know my name." And he proceeded to pronounce it.

"Oh, dear, I can't say all that!" said his companion with a laugh. But by this time they had come up to Mrs. Miller, who, as they drew near, walked to the parapet of the garden and leaned upon it, looking intently at the lake and turning her back to them. "Mother!" said the young girl in a tone of decision. Upon this the elder lady turned round. "Mr. Winterbourne," said Miss Daisy Miller, introducing the young man very frankly and prettily. "Common," she was, as Mrs. Costello had pronounced her; yet it was a wonder to Winterbourne that, with her commonness, she had a singularly delicate grace.

Her mother was a small, spare, light person, with a wandering eye, a very exiguous nose, and a large forehead, decorated with a certain amount of thin, much frizzled hair. Like her daughter, Mrs. Miller was dressed with extreme elegance; she had enormous diamonds in her ears. So far as Winterbourne could observe, she gave him no greeting—she certainly was not looking at him. Daisy was near her, pulling her shawl straight. "What are you doing, poking round here?" this young lady inquired, but by no means with that harshness of accent which her choice of words may imply.

"I don't know," said her mother, turning toward the lake again.

"I shouldn't think you'd want that shawl!" Daisy exclaimed.

"Well I do!" her mother answered with a little laugh.

"Did you get Randolph to go to bed?" asked the young girl.

"No; I couldn't induce him," said Mrs. Miller very gently. "He wants to talk to the waiter. He likes to talk to that waiter."

"I was telling Mr. Winterbourne," the young girl went on; and to the young man's ear her tone might have indicated that she had been uttering his name all her life.

"Oh, yes!" said Winterbourne; "I have the pleasure of knowing your son."

Randolph's mamma was silent; she turned her attention to the lake. But at last she spoke. "Well, I don't see how he lives!"

"Anyhow, it isn't so bad as it was at Dover," said Daisy Miller.

"And what occurred at Dover?" Winterbourne asked.

"He wouldn't go to bed at all. I guess he sat up all night in the public parlor. He wasn't in bed at twelve o'clock: I know that."

"It was half-past twelve," declared Mrs. Miller with mild emphasis.

"Does he sleep much during the day?" Winterbourne demanded.

"I guess he doesn't sleep much," Daisy rejoined.

"I wish he would!" said her mother. "It seems as if he couldn't."

"I think he's real tiresome," Daisy pursued.

Then, for some moments, there was silence. "Well, Daisy Miller," said the elder lady, presently, "I shouldn't think you'd want to talk against your own brother!"

"Well, he IS tiresome, Mother," said Daisy, quite without the asperity of a retort.

"He's only nine," urged Mrs. Miller.

"Well, he wouldn't go to that castle," said the young girl. "I'm going there with Mr. Winterbourne."

To this announcement, very placidly made, Daisy's mamma offered no response. Winterbourne took for granted that she deeply disapproved of the projected excursion; but he said to himself that she was a simple, easily managed person, and that a few deferential protestations would take the edge from her displeasure. "Yes," he began; "your daughter has kindly allowed me the honor of being her guide."

Mrs. Miller's wandering eyes attached themselves, with a sort of appealing air, to Daisy, who, however, strolled a few steps farther, gently humming to herself. "I presume you will go in the cars," said her mother.

"Yes, or in the boat," said Winterbourne.

"Well, of course, I don't know," Mrs. Miller rejoined. "I have never been to that castle."

"It is a pity you shouldn't go," said Winterbourne, beginning to feel reassured as to her opposition. And yet he was quite prepared to find that, as a matter of course, she meant to accompany her daughter.

"We've been thinking ever so much about going," she pursued; "but it seems as if we couldn't. Of course Daisy—she wants to go round. But there's a lady here—I don't know her name—she says she shouldn't think we'd want to go to see castles *here*; she should think we'd want to wait till we got to Italy. It seems as if there would be so many there," continued Mrs. Miller with an air of increasing confidence. "Of course we only want to see the principal ones. We visited several in England," she presently added.

"Ah yes! in England there are beautiful castles," said Winterbourne. "But Chillon here, is very well worth seeing."

"Well, if Daisy feels up to it—" said Mrs. Miller, in a tone impregnated with a sense of the magnitude of the enterprise. "It seems as if there was nothing she wouldn't undertake."

"Oh, I think she'll enjoy it!" Winterbourne declared. And he desired more and more to make it a certainty that he was to have the privilege of a tete-a-tete with the young lady, who was still strolling along in front of them, softly vocalizing. "You are not disposed, madam," he inquired, "to undertake it yourself?"

Daisy's mother looked at him an instant askance, and then walked forward in silence. Then—"I guess she had better go alone," she said simply. Winterbourne observed to himself that this was a very different type of maternity from that of the vigilant matrons who massed themselves in the forefront of social intercourse in the dark old city at the other end of the lake. But his meditations were interrupted by hearing his name very distinctly pronounced by Mrs. Miller's unprotected daughter.

"Mr. Winterbourne!" murmured Daisy.

"Mademoiselle!" said the young man.

"Don't you want to take me out in a boat?"

"At present?" he asked.

"Of course!" said Daisy.

"Well, Annie Miller!" exclaimed her mother.

"I beg you, madam, to let her go," said Winterbourne ardently; for he had never yet enjoyed the sensation of guiding through the summer starlight a skiff freighted with a fresh and beautiful young girl.

"I shouldn't think she'd want to," said her mother. "I should think she'd rather go indoors."

"I'm sure Mr. Winterbourne wants to take me," Daisy declared. "He's so awfully devoted!"

"I will row you over to Chillon in the starlight."

"I don't believe it!" said Daisy.

"Well!" ejaculated the elder lady again.

"You haven't spoken to me for half an hour," her daughter went on.

"I have been having some very pleasant conversation with your mother," said Winterbourne.

"Well, I want you to take me out in a boat!" Daisy repeated. They had all stopped, and she had turned round and was looking at Winterbourne. Her face wore a charming smile, her pretty eyes were gleaming, she was swinging her great fan about. No; it's impossible to be prettier than that, thought Winterbourne.

"There are half a dozen boats moored at that landing place," he said, pointing to certain steps which descended from the garden to the lake. "If you will do me the honor to accept my arm, we will go and select one of them."

Daisy stood there smiling; she threw back her head and gave a little, light laugh. "I like a gentleman to be formal!" she declared.

"I assure you it's a formal offer."

"I was bound I would make you say something," Daisy went on.

"You see, it's not very difficult," said Winterbourne. "But I am afraid you are chaffing me."

"I think not, sir," remarked Mrs. Miller very gently.

"Do, then, let me give you a row," he said to the young girl.

"It's quite lovely, the way you say that!" cried Daisy.

"It will be still more lovely to do it."

"Yes, it would be lovely!" said Daisy. But she made no movement to accompany him; she only stood there laughing.

"I should think you had better find out what time it is," interposed her mother.

"It is eleven o'clock, madam," said a voice, with a foreign accent, out of the neighboring darkness; and Winterbourne, turning, perceived the florid personage who was in attendance upon the two ladies. He had apparently just approached.

"Oh, Eugenio," said Daisy, "I am going out in a boat!"

Eugenio bowed. "At eleven o'clock, mademoiselle?"

"I am going with Mr. Winterbourne—this very minute."

"Do tell her she can't," said Mrs. Miller to the courier.

"I think you had better not go out in a boat, mademoiselle," Eugenio declared.

Winterbourne wished to Heaven this pretty girl were not so familiar with her courier; but he said nothing.

"I suppose you don't think it's proper!" Daisy exclaimed. "Eugenio doesn't think anything's proper."

"I am at your service," said Winterbourne.

"Does mademoiselle propose to go alone?" asked Eugenio of Mrs. Miller.

"Oh, no; with this gentleman!" answered Daisy's mamma.

The courier looked for a moment at Winterbourne—the latter thought he was smiling—and then, solemnly, with a bow, "As mademoiselle pleases!" he said.

"Oh, I hoped you would make a fuss!" said Daisy. "I don't care to go now."

"I myself shall make a fuss if you don't go," said Winterbourne.

"That's all I want—a little fuss!" And the young girl began to laugh again.

"Mr. Randolph has gone to bed!" the courier announced frigidly.

"Oh, Daisy; now we can go!" said Mrs. Miller.

Daisy turned away from Winterbourne, looking at him, smiling and fanning herself. "Good night," she said; "I hope you are disappointed, or disgusted, or something!"

He looked at her, taking the hand she offered him. "I am puzzled," he answered.

"Well, I hope it won't keep you awake!" she said very smartly; and, under the escort of the privileged Eugenio, the two ladies passed toward the house.

Winterbourne stood looking after them; he was indeed puzzled. He lingered beside the lake for a quarter of an hour, turning over the mystery of the young girl's sudden familiarities and caprices. But the only very definite conclusion he came to was that he should enjoy deucedly "going off" with her somewhere.

Mrs. Miller and her courier broke off from Daisy on the way back to the house, making their excuses about seeing the sunflowers swaying in the breeze in the lights of the hotel. Mrs. Miller had spotted a patch earlier in the day, and wanted to "show him how moving they must be when they were the only suns in the sky." Of course, Mrs. Miller hadn't ever cared for flowers as much as she could pluck one with her toes. The instant they were away from Daisy, her courier became her beloved Eugenie. Often, they enjoyed touching each other in their warmest places in front of the fireplace window, as the view of the other tourists made Mrs. Miller exceptionally vivacious.

This time, she pinched him by his wrist and dragged him to the beach tents, deserted by night but for a few nesting chaffinches. She hastily tied the canvas door shut, then unfastened his breeches and pulled them down to his ankles to free his magnificent cock. She sank to her knees, her mouth watering, aching for him. She let one hand delicately cup his balls. With great care, she let her tongue languorously move over his manhood from her fingertips to the tip of his prick, keeping his shaft in a viselike grip, and then dragging her tongue back again. When she was certain he could not take any more torture, she slapped his cock into her mouth and sucked it until the sides of her mouth swelled, like its contents, to accommodate him. Eugenio, normally so straight-backed unless in her private company, squirmed and stifled a soft exclamation in order to avoid disturbing the retiring hotel guests. In minutes, he tensed and shot his seed into her open mouth.

Overflowing, shiny fluid dripped down slowly from his prick onto her mouth and chin, and she let the same languorous tongue, (which made her Eugenie incredibly horny after every week-end breakfast), fetch the remaining seed. A glistening drop remained on his prick, to which she remarked she had better save her appetite for later. Mrs. Miller then rose from her knees, adjusted her dress, and laughingly took her courier back to the house.

Two days afterward, Winterbourne went off with Daisy to the Castle of Chillon. He waited for her in the large hall of the hotel, where the couriers, the servants, the foreign tourists, were lounging about and staring. It was not the place he should have chosen, but she had appointed it. She came tripping downstairs, buttoning her long gloves, and squeezing her folded parasol against her pretty figure, dressed in the perfection of a soberly elegant traveling costume. Winterbourne was a man of imagination and, as our ancestors used to say, sensibility; as he looked at her dress and, on the great staircase, her little rapid, confiding step, he felt as if there were something romantic going forward.

He could have believed he was going to elope with her. He passed out with her among all the idle people that were assembled there; they were all looking at her very hard; she had begun to chatter as soon as she joined him. Winterbourne's preference had been that they should be conveyed to Chillon in a carriage; but she expressed a lively wish to go in the little steamer; she declared that she had a passion for steamboats. There was always such a lovely breeze upon the water, and you saw such lots of people. The sail was not long, but Winterbourne's companion found time to say a great many things. To the young man himself their little excursion was so much of an escapade—an adventure—that, even allowing for her habitual sense of freedom, he had some expectation of seeing her regard it in the same way. But it must be confessed that, in this particular, he was disappointed.

Daisy Miller was extremely animated, she was in charming spirits; but she was apparently not at all excited; she was not fluttered; she avoided neither his eyes nor those of anyone else; she blushed neither when she looked at him nor when she felt that people were looking at her. People continued to look at her a great deal, and Winterbourne took much satisfaction in his pretty companion's distinguished air. He had been a little afraid that she would talk loud, laugh overmuch, and even, perhaps, desire to move about the boat a good deal. But he quite forgot his fears; he sat smiling, with his eyes upon her face, while, without moving from her place, she delivered herself of a great number of original reflections. It was the most charming garrulity he had ever heard. He had assented to the idea that she was "common"; but was she so, after all, or was he simply getting used to her commonness? Her conversation was chiefly of what metaphysicians term the objective cast, but every now and then it took a subjective turn.

"What on *earth* are you so grave about?" she suddenly demanded, fixing her agreeable eyes upon Winterbourne's.

"Am I grave?" he asked. "I had an idea I was grinning from ear to ear."

"You look as if you were taking me to a funeral. If that's a grin, your ears are very near together."

"Should you like me to dance a hornpipe on the deck?"

"Pray do, and I'll carry round your hat. It will pay the expenses of our journey."

"I never was better pleased in my life," murmured Winterbourne.

She looked at him a moment and then burst into a little laugh. "I like to make you say those things! You're a queer mixture!"

In the castle, after they had landed, the subjective element decidedly prevailed. Daisy tripped about the vaulted chambers, rustled her skirts in the corkscrew staircases, flirted back with a pretty little cry and a shudder from the edge of the oubliettes, and turned a singularly well-shaped ear to everything that Winterbourne told her about the place. But he saw that she cared very little for feudal antiquities and that the dusky traditions of Chillon made but a slight impression upon her. They had the good fortune to have been able to walk about without other companionship than that of the custodian; and Winterbourne arranged with this functionary that they should not be hurried—that they should linger and pause wherever they chose. The custodian interpreted the bargain generously—Winterbourne, on his side, had been generous—and ended by leaving them quite to themselves. Miss Miller's observations were not remarkable for logical consistency; for anything she wanted to say she was sure to find a pretext. She found a great many pretexts in the rugged embrasures of Chillon for asking Winterbourne sudden questions about himself—his family, his previous history, his tastes, his habits, his intentions—and for supplying information upon corresponding points in her own personality. Of her own tastes, habits, and intentions Miss Miller was prepared to give the most definite, and indeed the most favorable account.

"Well, I hope you know enough!" she said to her companion, after he had told her the history of the unhappy Bonivard. "I never saw a man that knew so much!" The history of Bonivard had evidently, as they say, gone into one ear and out of the other. But Daisy went on to say that she wished Winterbourne would travel with them and "go round" with them; they might know something, in that case. "Don't you want to come and teach Randolph?" she asked. Winterbourne said that nothing could possibly please him so much, but that he had unfortunately other occupations. "Other occupations? I don't believe it!" said Miss Daisy. "What do you mean? You are not in business." The young man admitted that he was not in business; but he had engagements which, even within a day or two, would force him to go back to

Geneva. "Oh, bother!" she said; "I don't believe it!" and she began to talk about something else. But a few moments later, when he was pointing out to her the pretty design of an antique fireplace, she broke out irrelevantly, "You don't mean to say you are going back to Geneva?"

"It is a melancholy fact that I shall have to return to Geneva tomorrow."

"Well, Mr. Winterbourne," said Daisy, "I think you're horrid!"

"Oh, don't say such dreadful things!" said Winterbourne— "just at the last!"

"The last!" cried the young girl; "I call it the first. I have half a mind to leave you here and go straight back to the hotel alone." And for the next ten minutes she did nothing but call him horrid. Poor Winterbourne was fairly bewildered; no young lady had as yet done him the honor to be so agitated by the announcement of his movements. His companion, after this, ceased to pay any attention to the curiosities of Chillon or the beauties of the lake; she opened fire upon the mysterious charmer in Geneva whom she appeared to have instantly taken it for granted that he was hurrying back to see.

How did Miss Daisy Miller know that there was a charmer in Geneva? Winterbourne, who denied the existence of such a person, was quite unable to discover, and he was divided between amazement at the rapidity of her induction and amusement at the frankness of her persiflage. She seemed to him, in all this, an extraordinary mixture of innocence and crudity. "Does she never allow you more than three days at a time?" asked Daisy ironically. "Doesn't she give you a vacation in summer? There's no one so hard worked but they can get leave to go off somewhere at this season. I suppose, if you stay another day, she'll come after you in the boat. Do wait over till Friday, and I will go down to the landing to see her arrive!" Winterbourne began to think he had been wrong to feel disappointed in the temper in which the young lady had embarked. If he had missed the personal accent, the personal accent was now making its appearance. It sounded very distinctly, at last, in her telling him she would stop "teasing" him if he would promise her solemnly to come down to Rome in the winter.

"That's not a difficult promise to make," said Winterbourne. "My aunt has taken an apartment in Rome for the winter and has already asked me to come and see her."

"I don't want you to come for your aunt," said Daisy; "I want you to come for me." And this was the only allusion that the young man was ever to hear her make to his invidious kinswoman. He declared that, at any rate, he would certainly come. After this Daisy stopped teasing. Winterbourne took a carriage, and they drove back to Vevey in the dusk; the young girl was very quiet.

In the evening Winterbourne mentioned to Mrs. Costello that he had spent the afternoon at Chillon with Miss Daisy Miller.

"The Americans—of the courier?" asked this lady.

"Ah, happily," said Winterbourne, "the courier stayed at home."

"She went with you all alone?"

"All alone."

Mrs. Costello sniffed a little at her smelling bottle. "And that," she exclaimed, "is the young person whom you wanted me to know!"

PART II

Winterbourne, who had returned to Geneva the day after his excursion to Chillon, went to Rome toward the end of January. His aunt had been established there for several weeks, and he had received a couple of letters from her. "Those people you were so devoted to last summer at Vevey have turned up here, courier and all," she wrote. "They seem to have made several acquaintances, but the courier continues to be the most intime. The young lady, however, is also very intimate with some third-rate Italians, with whom she rackets about in a way that makes much talk. Bring me that pretty novel of Cherbuliez's—Paule Mere—and don't come later than the 23rd."

In the natural course of events, Winterbourne, on arriving in Rome, would presently have ascertained Mrs. Miller's address at the American banker's and have gone to pay his compliments to Miss Daisy. "After what happened at Vevey, I think I may certainly call upon them," he said to Mrs. Costello.

"If, after what happens—at Vevey and everywhere—you desire to keep up the acquaintance, you are very welcome. Of course a man may know everyone. Men are welcome to the privilege!"

"Pray what is it that happens—here, for instance?" Winterbourne demanded.

"The girl goes about alone with her foreigners. As to what happens further, you must apply elsewhere for information. She has picked up half a dozen of the regular Roman fortune hunters, and she takes them about to people's houses. When she comes to a party she brings with her a gentleman with a good deal of manner and a wonderful mustache."

"And where is the mother?"

"I haven't the least idea. They are very dreadful people."

Winterbourne meditated a moment. "They are very ignorant—very innocent only. Depend upon it they are not bad."

"They are hopelessly vulgar," said Mrs. Costello. "Whether or no being hopelessly vulgar is being 'bad' is a question for the metaphysicians. They are bad enough to dislike, at any rate; and for this short life that is quite enough."

The news that Daisy Miller was surrounded by half a dozen wonderful mustaches checked Winterbourne's impulse to go straightway to see her. He had, perhaps, not definitely flattered himself that he had made an ineffaceable impression upon her heart, but he was annoyed at hearing of a state of affairs so little in harmony with an image that had lately flitted in and out of his own meditations; the image of a very pretty girl looking out of an old Roman window and asking herself urgently when Mr. Winterbourne would arrive. If, however, he determined to wait a little before reminding Miss Miller of his claims to her consideration, he went very soon to call upon two or three other friends.

One of these friends was an American lady who had spent several winters at Geneva, where she had placed her children at school. She was a very accomplished woman, and she lived in the Via Gregoriana. Winterbourne found her in a little crimson drawing room on a third floor; the room was filled with southern sunshine. He had not been there ten minutes when the servant came in, announcing "Madame Mila!" This announcement was presently followed by the entrance of little Randolph Miller, who stopped in the middle of the room and stood staring at Winterbourne. An instant later his pretty sister crossed the threshold; and then, after a considerable interval, Mrs. Miller slowly advanced.

"I know you!" said Randolph.

"I'm sure you know a great many things," exclaimed Winterbourne, taking him by the hand. "How is your education coming on?"

Daisy was exchanging greetings very prettily with her hostess, but when she heard Winterbourne's voice she quickly turned her head. "Well, I declare!" she said.

"I told you I should come, you know," Winterbourne rejoined, smiling.

"Well, I didn't believe it," said Miss Daisy.

"I am much obliged to you," laughed the young man.

"You might have come to see me!" said Daisy.

"I arrived only yesterday."

"I don't believe that!" the young girl declared.

Winterbourne turned with a protesting smile to her mother, but this lady evaded his glance, and, seating herself, fixed her eyes upon her son. "We've got a bigger place than this," said Randolph. "It's all gold on the walls."

Mrs. Miller turned uneasily in her chair. "I told you if I were to bring you, you would say something!" she murmured.

"I told *you*!" Randolph exclaimed. "I tell *you*, sir!" he added jocosely, giving Winterbourne a thump on the knee. "It *is* bigger, too!"

Daisy had entered upon a lively conversation with her hostess; Winterbourne judged it becoming to address a few words to her mother. "I hope you have been well since we parted at Vevey," he said.

Mrs. Miller now certainly looked at him—at his chin. "Not very well, sir," she answered.

"She's got the dyspepsia," said Randolph. "I've got it too. Father's got it. I've got it most!"

This announcement, instead of embarrassing Mrs. Miller, seemed to relieve her. "I suffer from the liver," she said. "I think it's this climate;

it's less bracing than Schenectady, especially in the winter season. I don't know whether you know we reside at Schenectady. I was saying to Daisy that I certainly hadn't found any one like Dr. Davis, and I didn't believe I should. Oh, at Schenectady he stands first; they think everything of him. He has so much to do, and yet there was nothing he wouldn't do for me. He said he never saw anything like my dyspepsia, but he was bound to cure it. I'm sure there was nothing he wouldn't try. He was just going to try something new when we came off. Mr. Miller wanted Daisy to see Europe for herself. But I wrote to Mr. Miller that it seems as if I couldn't get on without Dr. Davis. At Schenectady he stands at the very top; and there's a great deal of sickness there, too. It affects my sleep."

Winterbourne had a good deal of pathological gossip with Dr. Davis's patient, during which Daisy chattered unremittingly to her own companion. The young man asked Mrs. Miller how she was pleased with Rome. "Well, I must say I am disappointed," she answered. "We had heard so much about it; I suppose we had heard too much. But we couldn't help that. We had been led to expect something different."

"Ah, wait a little, and you will become very fond of it," said Winterbourne.

"I hate it worse and worse every day!" cried Randolph.

"You are like the infant Hannibal," said Winterbourne.

"No, I ain't!" Randolph declared at a venture.

"You are not much like an infant," said his mother. "But we have seen places," she resumed, "that I should put a long way before Rome." And in reply to Winterbourne's interrogation, "There's Zurich," she concluded, "I think Zurich is lovely; and we hadn't heard half so much about it."

"The best place we've seen is the City of Richmond!" said Randolph.

"He means the ship," his mother explained. "We crossed in that ship. Randolph had a good time on the City of Richmond."

"It's the best place I've seen," the child repeated. "Only it was turned the wrong way."

"Well, we've got to turn the right way some time," said Mrs. Miller with a little laugh. Winterbourne expressed the hope that her daughter at least found some gratification in Rome, and she declared that Daisy was quite carried away. "It's on account of the society—the society's splendid. She goes round everywhere; she has made a great number of acquaintances. Of course she goes round more than I do. I must say they have been very sociable; they have taken her right in. And then she knows a great many gentlemen. Oh, she thinks there's nothing like Rome. Of course, it's a great deal pleasanter for a young lady if she knows plenty of gentlemen."

By this time Daisy had turned her attention again to Winterbourne. "I've been telling Mrs. Walker how mean you were!" the young girl announced.

"And what is the evidence you have offered?" asked Winterbourne, rather annoyed at Miss Miller's want of appreciation of the zeal of an admirer who on his way down to Rome had stopped neither at Bologna nor at Florence, simply because of a certain sentimental impatience. He remembered that a cynical compatriot had once told him that American women— the pretty ones, and this gave a largeness to the axiom—were at once the most exacting in the world and the least endowed with a sense of indebtedness.

"Why, you were awfully mean at Vevey," said Daisy. "You wouldn't do anything. You wouldn't stay there when I asked you."

"My dearest young lady," cried Winterbourne, with eloquence, "have I come all the way to Rome to encounter your reproaches?"

"Just hear him say that!" said Daisy to her hostess, giving a twist to a bow on this lady's dress. "Did you ever hear anything so quaint?"

"So quaint, my dear?" murmured Mrs. Walker in the tone of a partisan of Winterbourne.

"Well, I don't know," said Daisy, fingering Mrs. Walker's ribbons. "Mrs. Walker, I want to tell you something."

"Mother-r," interposed Randolph, with his rough ends to his words, "I tell you you've got to go. Eugenio'll raise—something!"

"I'm not afraid of Eugenio," said Daisy with a toss of her head. "Look here, Mrs. Walker," she went on, "you know I'm coming to your party."

"I am delighted to hear it."

"I've got a lovely dress!"

"I am very sure of that."

"But I want to ask a favor—permission to bring a friend."

"I shall be happy to see any of your friends," said Mrs. Walker, turning with a smile to Mrs. Miller.

"Oh, they are not my friends," answered Daisy's mamma, smiling shyly in her own fashion. "I never spoke to them."

"It's an intimate friend of mine—Mr. Giovanelli," said Daisy without a tremor in her clear little voice or a shadow on her brilliant little face.

Mrs. Walker was silent a moment; she gave a rapid glance at Winterbourne. "I shall be glad to see Mr. Giovanelli," she then said.

"He's an Italian," Daisy pursued with the prettiest serenity. "He's a great friend of mine; he's the handsomest man in the world—except Mr. Winterbourne! He knows plenty of Italians, but he wants to know some Americans. He thinks ever so much of Americans. He's tremendously clever. He's perfectly lovely!"

It was settled that this brilliant personage should be brought to Mrs. Walker's party, and then Mrs. Miller prepared to take her leave. "I guess we'll go back to the hotel," she said.

"You may go back to the hotel, Mother, but I'm going to take a walk," said Daisy.

"She's going to walk with Mr. Giovanelli," Randolph proclaimed.

"I am going to the Pincio," said Daisy, smiling.

"Alone, my dear—at this hour?" Mrs. Walker asked. The afternoon was drawing to a close—it was the hour for the throng of carriages and of contemplative pedestrians. "I don't think it's safe, my dear," said Mrs. Walker.

"Neither do I," subjoined Mrs. Miller. "You'll get the fever, as sure as you live. Remember what Dr. Davis told you!"

"Give her some medicine before she goes," said Randolph.

The company had risen to its feet; Daisy, still showing her pretty teeth, bent over and kissed her hostess. "Mrs. Walker, you are too perfect," she said. "I'm not going alone; I am going to meet a friend."

"Your friend won't keep you from getting the fever," Mrs. Miller observed.

"Is it Mr. Giovanelli?" asked the hostess.

Winterbourne was watching the young girl; at this question his attention quickened. She stood there, smiling and smoothing her bonnet ribbons; she glanced at Winterbourne. Then, while she glanced and smiled, she answered, without a shade of hesitation, "Mr. Giovanelli—the beautiful Giovanelli."

"My dear young friend," said Mrs. Walker, taking her hand pleadingly, "don't walk off to the Pincio at this hour to meet a beautiful Italian."

"Well, he speaks English," said Mrs. Miller.

"Gracious me!" Daisy exclaimed, "I don't mean to do anything improper. There's an easy way to settle it." She continued to glance at Winterbourne. "The Pincio is only a hundred yards distant; and if Mr. Winterbourne were as polite as he pretends, he would offer to walk with me!"

Winterbourne's politeness hastened to affirm itself, and the young girl gave him gracious leave to accompany her. They passed downstairs before her mother, and at the door Winterbourne perceived Mrs. Miller's carriage drawn up, with the ornamental courier whose acquaintance he had made at Vevey seated within. "Goodbye, Eugenio!" cried Daisy; "I'm going to take a walk." The distance from the Via Gregoriana to the beautiful garden at the other end of the Pincian Hill is, in fact, rapidly traversed. As the day was splendid, however, and the concourse of vehicles, walkers, and loungers numerous, the young Americans found their progress much delayed. This fact was highly agreeable to Winterbourne, in spite of his consciousness of his singular situation.

Meanwhile, Eugenio and Mrs. Miller were completely unaware of Winterbourne's progress or impediment, having busied themselves with placating Eugenio's never-ceasing lust for semiprivate tête-à-têtes, or in this instance, tête-bêches: Their heads were at each other's wet bits in the closed carriage. Mrs. Miller was in her own heaven; who could blame her for allowing a gentleman to walk her daughter to the gardens? Eugenio was flitting his tongue in a manner so agreeable that her oversized nipples were hardening, and he loved the sight of her pulling away to delay her own pleasure. Meanwhile, his trousers were around his ankles and he was bracing his legs against the sides of the carriage in order to fit sideways into the narrow seats, while Mrs. Miller's skirts covered the top half of his body entirely as she worked at the only job she had ever known, her fingers grasping the shaft of his prick and her tongue skimming the surface of the tip in rhythm to his tongue on her clit.

Meanwhile, the slow-moving, idly gazing Roman crowd bestowed much attention upon the extremely pretty young foreign lady who was passing through it upon Winterbourne's arm; and he wondered what on earth had been in Daisy's mind when she proposed to expose herself, unattended, to its appreciation. His own mission, to her sense, apparently, was to consign her to the hands of Mr. Giovanelli; but Winterbourne, at once annoyed and gratified, resolved that he would do no such thing.

"Why haven't you been to see me?" asked Daisy. "You can't get out of that."

"I have had the honor of telling you that I have only just stepped out of the train."

"You must have stayed in the train a good while after it stopped!" cried the young girl with her little laugh. "I suppose you were asleep. You have had time to go to see Mrs. Walker."

"I knew Mrs. Walker—" Winterbourne began to explain.

"I know where you knew her. You knew her at Geneva. She told me so. Well, you knew me at Vevey. That's just as good. So you ought to have come." She asked him no other question than this; she began to prattle about her own affairs. "We've got splendid rooms at the hotel; Eugenio says they're the best rooms in Rome. We are going to stay all winter, if we don't die of the fever; and I guess we'll stay then. It's a great deal nicer than I thought; I thought it would be fearfully quiet; I was sure it would be awfully poky. I was sure we should be going round all the time with one of those dreadful old men that explain about the pictures and things. But we only had about a week of that, and now I'm enjoying myself. I know ever so many people, and they are all so charming. The society's extremely select. There are all kinds—English, and Germans, and Italians. I think I like the English best. I like their style of conversation. But there are some lovely Americans. I never saw anything so hospitable. There's something or other every day. There's not much dancing; but I must say I never thought dancing was everything. I was always fond of conversation. I guess I shall have plenty at Mrs. Walker's, her rooms are so small." When they had passed the gate of the Pincian Gardens, Miss Miller began to wonder where Mr. Giovanelli might be. "We had better go straight to that place in front," she said, "where you look at the view."

"I certainly shall not help you to find him," Winterbourne declared.

"Then I shall find him without you," cried Miss Daisy.

"You certainly won't leave me!" cried Winterbourne.

She burst into her little laugh. "Are you afraid you'll get lost— or run over? But there's Giovanelli, leaning against that tree. He's staring at the women in the carriages: did you ever see anything so cool?"

Winterbourne perceived at some distance a little man standing with folded arms nursing his cane. He had a handsome face, an artfully poised hat, a glass in one eye, and a nosegay in his buttonhole. Winterbourne looked at him a moment and then said, "Do you mean to speak to that man?"

"Do I mean to speak to him? Why, you don't suppose I mean to communicate by signs?"

"Pray understand, then," said Winterbourne, "that I intend to remain with you."

Daisy stopped and looked at him, without a sign of troubled consciousness in her face, with nothing but the presence of her charming eyes and her happy dimples. "Well, she's a cool one!" thought the young man.

"I don't like the way you say that," said Daisy. "It's too imperious."

"I beg your pardon if I say it wrong. The main point is to give you an idea of my meaning."

The young girl looked at him more gravely, but with eyes that were prettier than ever. "I have never allowed a gentleman to dictate to me, or to interfere with anything I do."

"I think you have made a mistake," said Winterbourne. "You should sometimes listen to a gentleman—the right one."

Daisy began to laugh again. "I do nothing but listen to gentlemen!" she exclaimed. "Tell me if Mr. Giovanelli is the right one?"

The gentleman with the nosegay in his bosom had now perceived our two friends, and was approaching the young girl with obsequious rapidity. He bowed to Winterbourne as well as to the latter's companion; he had a brilliant smile, an intelligent eye; Winterbourne thought him not a bad-looking fellow. But he nevertheless said to Daisy, "No, he's not the right one." Winterbourne would rather have dropped down to his knees and eaten an uncooked frog in front of them both, than let Giovanelli enjoy the mere scent, the radiating bodily warmth, of Daisy the way *he* did.

Frederick, you see, had developed a veritable addiction to touching Daisy in a way that seemed utterly harmless to the surrounding men, and in all probability to Daisy, but made Winterbourne twinge with guilt. When he accompanied her to the garden this day, her waspish arm in his, he was plagued by happy thoughts of suckling at her breast with the eagerness of a newborn calf, of slipping a half hand casually between her thighs as if he were reaching for buffet toast. However, interrupting his, by his own admission, comically improbable fantasy, were thoughts of Daisy looking at Giovanelli with but a single lustful gleam in her eye. This had never occurred, to his knowledge, but oh, what he would do if Giovanelli were the one to graze Daisy's arm with the deeper aim that Winterbourne had! The monster Giovanelli, with his lips chewing up Daisy's beautiful mouth, (Augh! His hands running all over her undeserving body!), would be slipping, bumbling, into her slick quim. No! Only Frederick belonged between those thighs, and he would see to *that*!

Daisy evidently had a natural talent for performing introductions; she mentioned the name of each of her companions to the other. She strolled alone with one of them on each side of her; Mr. Giovanelli, who spoke English very cleverly—Winterbourne afterward learned that he had practiced the idiom upon a great many American heiresses—addressed her a great deal of very polite nonsense; he was extremely urbane, and the young American, who said nothing, reflected upon that profundity of Italian cleverness which enables people to appear more gracious in proportion as they are more acutely disappointed. Giovanelli, of course, had counted upon something more intimate; he had not bargained for a party of three. But he kept his temper in a manner which suggested far-stretching intentions. Winterbourne flattered himself that he had taken his measure.

"He is not a gentleman," said the young American; "he is only a clever imitation of one. He is a music master, or a penny-a-liner, or a third-rate artist. D__n his good looks!" Mr. Giovanelli had certainly a very pretty face; but Winterbourne felt a superior indignation at his own lovely fellow countrywoman's not knowing the difference between a spurious gentleman and a real one. Giovanelli chattered and jested and made himself wonderfully agreeable. It was true that, if he was an imitation, the imitation was brilliant.

"Nevertheless," Winterbourne said to himself, "a nice girl ought to know!" And then he came back to the question whether this was, in fact, a nice girl. Would a nice girl, even allowing for her being a little American flirt, make a rendezvous with a presumably low-lived foreigner? The rendezvous in this case, indeed, had been in broad daylight and in the most crowded corner of Rome, but was it not impossible to regard the choice of these circumstances as a proof of extreme cynicism? Singular though it may seem, Winterbourne was vexed that the young girl, in joining her amoroso, should not appear more impatient of his own company, and he was vexed because of his inclination.

It was impossible to regard her as a perfectly well-conducted young lady; she was wanting in a certain indispensable delicacy. It would therefore simplify matters greatly to be able to treat her as the object of one of those sentiments which are called by romancers "lawless passions." That she should seem to wish to get rid of him would help him to think more lightly of her, and to be able to think more lightly of her would make her much less perplexing. But Daisy, on this occasion, continued to present herself as an inscrutable combination of audacity and innocence.

She had been walking some quarter of an hour, attended by her two cavaliers, and responding in a tone of very childish gaiety, as it seemed to Winterbourne, to the pretty speeches of Mr. Giovanelli, when a carriage that had detached itself from the revolving train drew up beside the path. At the same moment Winterbourne perceived that his friend Mrs. Walker—the lady whose house he had lately left—was seated in the vehicle and was beckoning to him. Leaving Miss Miller's side, he hastened to obey her summons. Mrs. Walker was flushed; she wore an excited air. "It is really too dreadful," she said. "That girl must not do this sort of thing. She must not walk here with you two men. Fifty people have noticed her."

Winterbourne raised his eyebrows. "I think it's a pity to make too much fuss about it."

"It's a pity to let the girl ruin herself!"

"She is very innocent," said Winterbourne.

"She's very crazy!" cried Mrs. Walker. "Did you ever see anything so imbecile as her mother? After you had all left me just now, I could not sit still for thinking of it. It seemed too pitiful, not even to attempt to save her. I ordered the carriage and put on my bonnet, and came here as quickly as possible. Thank Heaven I have found you!"

"What do you propose to do with us?" asked Winterbourne, smiling.

"To ask her to get in, to drive her about here for half an hour, so that the world may see she is not running absolutely wild, and then to take her safely home."

"I don't think it's a very happy thought," said Winterbourne; "but you can try."

Mrs. Walker tried. The young man went in pursuit of Miss Miller, who had simply nodded and smiled at his interlocutor in the carriage and had gone her way with her companion. Daisy, on learning that Mrs. Walker wished to speak to her, retraced her steps with a perfect good grace and with Mr. Giovanelli at her side. She declared that she was delighted to have a chance to present this gentleman to Mrs. Walker. She immediately achieved the introduction, and declared that she had never in her life seen anything so lovely as Mrs. Walker's carriage rug.

"I am glad you admire it," said this lady, smiling sweetly. "Will you get in and let me put it over you?"

"Oh, no, thank you," said Daisy. "I shall admire it much more as I see you driving round with it."

"Do get in and drive with me!" said Mrs. Walker.

"That would be charming, but it's so enchanting just as I am!" and Daisy gave a brilliant glance at the gentlemen on either side of her.

"It may be enchanting, dear child, but it is not the custom here," urged Mrs. Walker, leaning forward in her victoria, with her hands devoutly clasped.

"Well, it ought to be, then!" said Daisy. "If I didn't walk I should expire."

"You should walk with your mother, dear," cried the lady from Geneva, losing patience.

"With my mother dear!" exclaimed the young girl. Winterbourne saw that she scented interference. "My mother never walked ten steps in her life. And then, you know," she added with a laugh, "I am more than five years old."

"You are old enough to be more reasonable. You are old enough, dear Miss Miller, to be talked about."

Daisy looked at Mrs. Walker, smiling intensely. "Talked about? What do you mean?"

"Come into my carriage, and I will tell you."

Daisy turned her quickened glance again from one of the gentlemen beside her to the other. Mr. Giovanelli was bowing to and fro, rubbing down his gloves and laughing very agreeably; Winterbourne thought it a most unpleasant scene. "I don't think I want to know what you mean," said Daisy presently. "I don't think I should like it."

Winterbourne wished that Mrs. Walker would tuck in her carriage rug and drive away, but this lady did not enjoy being defied, as she afterward told him. "Should you prefer being thought a very reckless girl?" she demanded.

"Gracious!" exclaimed Daisy. She looked again at Mr. Giovanelli, then she turned to Winterbourne. There was a little pink flush in her cheek; she was tremendously pretty. "Does Mr. Winterbourne think," she asked slowly, smiling, throwing back her head, and glancing at him from head to foot, "that, to save my reputation, I ought to get into the carriage?"

Winterbourne colored; for an instant he hesitated greatly. It seemed so strange to hear her speak that way of her "reputation." But he himself, in fact, must speak in accordance with gallantry. The finest gallantry, here, was simply to tell her the truth; and the truth, for Winterbourne, as the few indications I have been able to give have made him known to the reader, was that Daisy Miller should take Mrs. Walker's advice. He looked at her exquisite prettiness, and then he said, very gently, "I think you should get into the carriage."

Daisy gave a violent laugh. "I never heard anything so stiff! If this is improper, Mrs. Walker," she pursued, "then I am all improper, and you must give me up. Goodbye; I hope you'll have a lovely ride!" and, with Mr. Giovanelli, who made a triumphantly obsequious salute, she turned away.

Mrs. Walker sat looking after her, and there were tears in Mrs. Walker's eyes. "Get in here, sir," she said to Winterbourne, indicating the place beside her. The young man answered that he felt bound to accompany Miss Miller, whereupon Mrs. Walker declared that if he refused her this favor she would never speak to him again. She was evidently in earnest. Winterbourne overtook Daisy and her companion, and, offering the young girl his hand, told her that Mrs. Walker had made an imperious claim upon his society. He expected that in answer she would say something rather free, something to commit herself still further to that "recklessness" from which Mrs. Walker had so charitably endeavored to dissuade her. But she only shook his hand, hardly looking at him, while Mr. Giovanelli bade him farewell with a too emphatic flourish of the hat.

Winterbourne was not in the best possible humor as he took his seat in Mrs. Walker's victoria. "That was not clever of you," he said candidly, while the vehicle mingled again with the throng of carriages.

"In such a case," his companion answered, "I don't wish to be clever; I wish to be *earnest!*"

"Well, your earnestness has only offended her and put her off."

"It has happened very well," said Mrs. Walker. "If she is so perfectly determined to compromise herself, the sooner one knows it the better; one can act accordingly."

"I suspect she meant no harm," Winterbourne rejoined.

"So I thought a month ago. But she has been going too far."

"What has she been doing?"

"Everything that is not done here. Flirting with any man she could pick up; sitting in corners with mysterious Italians; dancing all the evening with the same partners; receiving visits at eleven o'clock at night. Her mother goes away when visitors come."

"But her brother," said Winterbourne, laughing, "sits up till midnight."

"He must be edified by what he sees. I'm told that at their hotel everyone is talking about her, and that a smile goes round among all the servants when a gentleman comes and asks for Miss Miller."

"The servants be hanged!" said Winterbourne angrily. "The poor girl's only fault," he presently added, "is that she is very uncultivated."

"She is naturally indelicate," Mrs. Walker declared.

"Take that example this morning. How long had you known her at Vevey?"

"A couple of days."

"Fancy, then, her making it a personal matter that you should have left the place!"

Winterbourne was silent for some moments; then he said, "I suspect, Mrs. Walker, that you and I have lived too long at Geneva!" And he added a request that she should inform him with what particular design she had made him enter her carriage.

"I wished to beg you to cease your relations with Miss Miller—not to flirt with her—to give her no further opportunity to expose herself—to let her alone, in short."

"I'm afraid I can't do that," said Winterbourne. "I like her extremely."

"All the more reason that you shouldn't help her to make a scandal."

"There shall be nothing scandalous in my attentions to her."

"There certainly will be in the way she takes them. But I have said what I had on my conscience," Mrs. Walker pursued. "If you wish to rejoin the young lady I will put you down. Here, by the way, you have a chance."

The carriage was traversing that part of the Pincian Garden that overhangs the wall of Rome and overlooks the beautiful Villa Borghese. It is bordered by a large parapet, near which there are several seats. One of the seats at a distance was occupied by a gentleman and a lady, toward whom Mrs. Walker gave a toss of her head. At the same moment these persons rose and walked toward the parapet. Winterbourne had asked the coachman to stop; he now descended from the carriage. His companion looked at him a moment in silence; then, while he raised his hat, she drove majestically away.

Winterbourne stood there; he had turned his eyes toward Daisy and her cavalier. They evidently saw no one; they were too deeply occupied with each other. When they reached the low garden wall, they stood a moment looking off at the great flat-topped pine clusters of the Villa Borghese; then Giovanelli seated himself, familiarly, upon the broad ledge of the wall. The western sun in the opposite sky sent out a brilliant shaft through a couple of cloud bars, whereupon Daisy's companion took her parasol out of her hands and opened it. She came a little nearer, and he held the parasol over her; then, still holding it, he let it rest upon her shoulder, so that both of their heads were hidden from Winterbourne. This young man lingered a moment, then he began to walk. But he walked—not toward the couple with the parasol; toward the residence of his aunt, Mrs. Costello.

He flattered himself on the following day that there was no smiling among the servants when he, at least, asked for Mrs. Miller at her hotel. This lady and her daughter, however, were not at home; and on the next day after, repeating his visit, Winterbourne again had the misfortune not to find them. Mrs. Walker's party took place on the evening of the third day, and, in spite of the frigidity of his last interview with the hostess, Winterbourne was among the guests. Mrs. Walker was one of those American ladies who, while residing abroad, make a point, in their own phrase, of studying European society, and she had on this occasion collected several specimens of her diversely born fellow mortals to serve, as it were, as textbooks. When Winterbourne arrived, Daisy Miller was not there, but in a few moments he saw her mother come in alone, very shyly and ruefully. Mrs. Miller's hair above her exposed-looking temples was more frizzled than ever. As she approached Mrs. Walker, Winterbourne also drew near.

"You see, I've come all alone," said poor Mrs. Miller. "I'm so frightened; I don't know what to do. It's the first time I've ever been to a party alone, especially in this country. I wanted to bring Randolph or Eugenio, or someone, but Daisy just pushed me off by myself. I ain't used to going round alone."

"And does not your daughter intend to favor us with her society?" demanded Mrs. Walker impressively.

"Well, Daisy's all dressed," said Mrs. Miller with that accent of the dispassionate, if not of the philosophic, historian with which she always recorded the current incidents of her daughter's career. "She got dressed on purpose before dinner. But she's got a friend of hers there; that gentleman—the Italian—that she wanted to bring. They've got going at the piano; it seems as if they couldn't leave off. Mr. Giovanelli sings splendidly. But I guess they'll come before very long," concluded Mrs. Miller hopefully.

"I'm sorry she should come in that way," said Mrs. Walker.

"Well, I told her that there was no use in her getting dressed before dinner if she was going to wait three hours," responded Daisy's mamma. "I didn't see the use of her putting on such a dress as that to sit round with Mr. Giovanelli."

"This is most horrible!" said Mrs. Walker, turning away and addressing herself to Winterbourne. "Elle s'affiche. It's her revenge for my having ventured to remonstrate with her. When she comes, I shall not speak to her."

Mrs. Miller, of course, didn't admit the slightest fault to herself for sporting a particularly flattering low-cut silk dress over her décolletage, and neither did the gentlemen at the party for staring in her direction and giving her their winningest smiles. She knew her impeccably sewn lace bertha allowed for a lower neckline that would customarily be acceptable at parties such as these, but she enjoyed the eyes that were resting upon her, and allowed herself to smile back at them, giving Miss Walker cause to ignore her further and exhale a series of petulant sighs.

But Mrs. Miller was not a stranger to Italy, and her natural poco curante attitude would stave them off. She stole away from Miss Walker and knocked on the locked tearoom, where she found Eugenio alone. He guided her to a plush chair by the fire.

Mrs. Miller had known upon hiring Eugenio that he would be inclined to attempt to woo her. His eyes, hard and at times disapproving upon almost everyone else, always softened upon Mrs. Miller. There was no reason to disbelieve his intentions, as he had been the utmost example of servitude with the Millers since he and Mrs. Miller were teens, and he had saved Daisy numerous times from fever, plucked Randolph from extraordinary hiking precipices, and carried Mrs. Miller for seven miles when she had broken a toe in Schenectady.

He had whispered to her on the way to her house that night that he would carry her a thousand times over if she would only ask, and she had no choice but to believe him. Eugenio told Mrs. Miller, his fleur de lis, often that she was an astonishingly attractive woman, but that he had found a good deal, so to speak, because most other men were asinine and only had eyes for her breasts. Unfortunately for her, her husband was of that sort. Sensitive Eugenio though, saw endless delight in her noble and fiery hair, her face, her round waist; to him they were symbols of her undying womanhood.

Though they both attempted to keep their sensory delights shrouded in secrecy, at times the urge was too great to avoid exhibiting their affection, if only through the closed windows of third-floor Europe. And though Mrs. Miller knew that Eugenio would be ever the discreet gentleman should they agree to part ways from their physical domain over each other, she had no intention of disentangling herself, and as of then his hands were entangling themselves in her outer skirts. She immediately began to giggle from this fervent accrual of silk under his arms. Confused and frustrated as pure, nonlubricious men usually are by the never-ending layers of fabric on their wives' drop-waists at first fumble, Eugenio reddened.

"Oh, my Eugenie!," taunted Mrs. Miller, "is the task not up to snuff? Shall I hire another courier, perhaps one more accustomed to the territory?" With that, her Eugenie's hands ripped down her petticoat, found her plump bottom, and gave it two satisfying smacks, sending delicious ripples through her body. "By George, I am the best d—n courier you've ever had, the *only* one you've *had*, and I have no intention of giving up my favorite duty, which is exploring the treats of your tight perineum."

He allowed his index finger to find her favorite spot. "Well, I guess you had better get to work then, shan't you, Signor Eugenio of the Good Flesh?" This 'good spot' that he had found was right between her quivering snatch and her small, feminine anus. Lately, he had tried to interest her more in the latter, but she would lose interest in seconds. This time, in front of the third-story window looking out into the beginning of the Spanish steps themselves, where men perhaps a hundred years prior had done the same, Eugenio couldn't believe his luck—she was letting his finger slowly screw its way into her forbidden hole—and she was smiling at this. "Thank you for bringing us the croissants this morning," said Mrs. Miller, in her matter-of-fact way. Her bland condescension continually angered Mr. Miller, but drew Eugenio even closer. To him it was sublime.

More fingers followed the first, and with a small flask of olive oil he seemed to procure by means of a happy miracle from his tight suit, he roughly shoved in three fingers, before filling her easy glove with his eager cock in the meantime.

Daisy came to the main party after eleven o'clock, after her mother returned to the hotel with Eugenio in tow, but she was not, on such an occasion, a young lady to wait to be spoken to. She rustled forward in radiant loveliness, smiling and chattering, carrying a large bouquet, and attended by Mr. Giovanelli.

Everyone stopped talking and turned and looked at her. She came straight to Mrs. Walker. "I'm afraid you thought I never was coming, so I sent mother off to tell you. I wanted to make Mr. Giovanelli practice some things before he came; you know he sings beautifully, and I want you to ask him to sing. This is Mr. Giovanelli; you know I introduced him to you; he's got the most lovely voice, and he knows the most charming set of songs. I made him go over them this evening on purpose; we had the greatest time at the hotel."

Of all this Daisy delivered herself with the sweetest, brightest audibleness, looking now at her hostess and now round the room, while she gave a series of little pats, round her shoulders, to the edges of her dress. "Is there anyone I know?" she asked.

"I think every one knows you!" said Mrs. Walker pregnantly, and she gave a very cursory greeting to Mr. Giovanelli. This gentleman bore himself gallantly. He smiled and bowed and showed his white teeth; he curled his mustaches and rolled his eyes and performed all the proper functions of a handsome Italian at an evening party. He sang very prettily half a dozen songs, though Mrs. Walker afterward declared that she had been quite unable to find out who asked him. It was apparently not Daisy who had given him his orders. Daisy sat at a distance from the piano, and though she had publicly, as it were, professed a high admiration for his singing, talked, not inaudibly, while it was going on.

"It's a pity these rooms are so small; we can't dance," she said to Winterbourne, as if she had seen him five minutes before.

"I am not sorry we can't dance," Winterbourne answered; "I don't dance."

"Of course you don't dance; you're too stiff," said Miss Daisy. "I hope you enjoyed your drive with Mrs. Walker!"

"No. I didn't enjoy it; I preferred walking with you."

"We paired off: that was much better," said Daisy. "But did you ever hear anything so cool as Mrs. Walker's wanting me to get into her carriage and drop poor Mr. Giovanelli, and under the pretext that it was proper? People have different ideas! It would have been most unkind; he had been talking about that walk for ten days."

"He should not have talked about it at all," said Winterbourne; "he would never have proposed to a young lady of this country to walk about the streets with him."

"About the streets?" cried Daisy with her pretty stare. "Where, then, would he have proposed to her to walk? The Pincio is not the streets, either; and I, thank goodness, am not a young lady of this country. The young ladies of this country have a dreadfully poky time of it, so far as I can learn; I don't see why I should change my habits for *them*."

"I am afraid your habits are those of a flirt," said Winterbourne gravely.

"Of course they are," she cried, giving him her little smiling stare again. "I'm a fearful, frightful flirt! Did you ever hear of a nice girl that was not? But I suppose you will tell me now that I am not a nice girl."

"You're a very nice girl; but I wish you would flirt with me, and me only," said Winterbourne.

"Ah! thank you—thank you very much; you are the last man I should think of flirting with. As I have had the pleasure of informing you, you are too stiff."

"You say that too often," said Winterbourne.

Daisy gave a delighted laugh. "If I could have the sweet hope of making you angry, I should say it again."

"Don't do that; when I am angry I'm stiffer than ever. But if you won't flirt with me, do cease, at least, to flirt with your friend at the piano; they don't understand that sort of thing here."

"I thought they understood nothing else!" exclaimed Daisy.

"Not in young unmarried women."

"It seems to me much more proper in young unmarried women than in old married ones," Daisy declared.

"Well," said Winterbourne, "when you deal with natives you must go by the custom of the place. Flirting is a purely American custom; it doesn't exist here. So when you show yourself in public with Mr. Giovanelli, and without your mother—"

"Gracious! poor Mother!" interposed Daisy.

"Though you may be flirting, Mr. Giovanelli is not; he means something else."

"He isn't preaching, at any rate," said Daisy with vivacity. "And if you want very much to know, we are neither of us flirting; we are too good friends for that: we are very intimate friends."

"Ah!" rejoined Winterbourne, "if you are in love with each other, it is another affair."

She had allowed him up to this point to talk so frankly that he had no expectation of shocking her by this ejaculation; but she immediately got up, blushing visibly, and leaving him to exclaim mentally that little American flirts were the queerest creatures in the world. "Mr. Giovanelli, at least," she said, giving her interlocutor a single glance, "never says such very disagreeable things to me."

Winterbourne was bewildered; he stood, staring. Mr. Giovanelli had finished singing. He left the piano and came over to Daisy. "Won't you come into the other room and have some tea?" he asked, bending before her with his ornamental smile.

Daisy turned to Winterbourne, beginning to smile again. He was still more perplexed, for this inconsequent smile made nothing clear, though it seemed to prove, indeed, that she had a sweetness and softness that reverted instinctively to the pardon of offenses. "It has never occurred to Mr. Winterbourne to offer me any tea," she said with her little tormenting manner.

"I have offered you advice," Winterbourne rejoined.

Daisy appeared to have had her fill of the repartee, and her neck pulsed for a millionth of a second as though shocked not only by the cruelty of Winterbourne's opinions, but through an unforeseen flurry of deep self-consciousness. Winterbourne rested his eyes upon her and dared to look left, making a slight motion to the now deserted antechamber, far past the hallways and bedrooms that might have been occupied. Daisy faltered before she completely regained her composure, which compelled her to sit, still and furious. Winterbourne excused himself on pretense of doing his business, and made a slow pace toward Miss Walker's bedroom just behind the aforementioned room.

As he strode past Miss Walker's delicately filigreed bench, he sat, giving his knee a pat and lighting himself a cigarette. That girl vexed him. He had made up his mind to leave the party, when one of the door handles gave, a slight twist. And the petite and splendid shoes of Daisy, solo, appeared to him. She walked up to Winterbourne so quickly that he reddened and turned deeply hot in the dark, the moonlight streaming in to illuminate her small soothing hands, now on his chest.

He had no choice but to be ecstatically clear with this maddening girl. "I would give my life to betroth myself to you in this very second," Winterbourne blurted, "*Je me suis entichée.* And yet it means nothing to you, doesn't it?" He was holding her now, tightly, and she was soft and breathless in his arms. She closed her eyes and he bent his head in, cautious. Their lips met in a kiss so sweet that Winterbourne almost choked. He smiled his mischievous grin and squeezed her waist, under little protest.

She was hot and skittish and he would never forget it. "Please demonstrate," said Daisy. "Pardon?" offered Winterbourne. Winterbourne had never expected a girl to challenge him thusly after he imagined himself in a good position to win her over for himself. He thought to himself that he would never have it again, and that he might prefer it that way. The way she had him how she wanted was almost criminal. Daisy let her hands creep behind his cutaway coat. Winterbourne froze. "Daisy, please. This is beyond the boundaries of any form of propriety. I *cannot* let you ruin yourself—your already precipitous place in society here. After all, you see that I am not stiff now, and—" Her hands slid around his waist and pulled him closer. His hands were on her hips now, firmly, and he was trembling.

"Winterbourne, I want you to prove you can *properly* ruin me, or I cannot ever be your wife. Show me you can take me and make me yours *now*. Put your hands on me the way I want you to, and I will betroth myself to you within a week and this small trespass won't be known. You are acting as if you have never touched a woman before. I know you know about the whores in the dingier parts of Europe."

At this, Winterbourne scoffed. "I wouldn't touch a woman I wasn't madly in love with. And that is the honest truth." Daisy scoffed. Winterbourne could not help himself now; he was a dog with lust for her. She sneered at him and he sneered back. He abruptly grabbed her small, waspy waist. He lowered her gently onto the chaise and she sat facing him. He knelt down in front of her and looked up. "Well?" said Daisy.

He moved next to her and immediately put his hands under her skirts. He adjusted his posture and his growing prick pressed into his pants with a pulsing urgency. He moved his fingers in a delicate and deliberate way up to her firm, round ass. He thought a perfect peach couldn't have been better formed. He grabbed her soft buttocks and pulled her down on top of him. She gave him a happy cry. "This is exactly what I want from you, you naughty man! I knew you were naughty, Frederick! Show me *more!*" cried Daisy, throwing her head back as she lifted her skirt entirely, facing him whilst on his lap. He picked her up, her well-formed legs wrapped tightly around his waist, and walked into the American-style pantry, almost tripping, and locking the door.

On a framed-velvet chair that one of Miss Walker's unfortunate minions had left behind that morning to fix the lightbulb, Daisy sat. She lifted up her skirts again, very matter-of-factly. Winterbourne knelt in front of her again and slyly reached a single finger under the wet right side of her washed-silk panties as she threw her head back and moaned. His prick wanted to enter her so badly it was aching and making him intensely uncomfortable by pressing itself into the crotch seam of his pants. She pressed her hand onto his and guided his hand to her hot slit.

She was grasping the curls on his head as he grinned up at her, slipping the fingers of his left hand into her and his right hand holding his manhood in a gardener's tightest grasp. She was now mildly perspiring, a delicate mist on her warm skin. It seemed to invite him in, and her body responded to the way his fingers moved in such a lovely way that he couldn't help but to pull her waist closer. He peeled her underskirts all the way down onto one of her smooth, firm legs and let his left fingers continue working into her. He'd never felt anything like this type of mad sexual frenzy for any other woman—he would have been ashamed if it didn't feel so delicious. He was doing it with pure love, of course, but he still felt so aroused—so naughty!—about this illicit encounter with her as if he *had* been with a whore in India.

His hands were digging into her firm ass again as if to absorb her very essence. He stood up abruptly and lifted her off, as the nymph had somehow managed to drop Winterbourne's pants to the floor in one fell swoop. She grabbed his shaft in a second quick movement. Winterbourne sat on the chair and beckoned her with a warm smile. She stood in front of him, now naked but for her underskirt gathered about her waist in her petite hands. He took one of these hands and pulled her in until she was facing him and sitting on his lap, straddling him. Cupping her face with one hand, he gently moved so his prick barely entered her aching quim. He then pushed into Daisy so he was inside of her to the wet hilt.

Both Winterbourne and Daisy let their minds give way to the indescribable pleasure they both felt as Daisy shoved his hot prick into her small, overwhelmed sex as far as her anatomy would allow, and rode him rather awkwardly and as roughly as she could manage.

She giggled in delight as she shoved her pretty breasts into his face, as Winterbourne licked them and smiled at his luck. He took over the rhythm and screwed his prick into her as they'd always wanted to from the moment they met. Frantically, dirtily, and as deeply as they could shove into each other. She didn't think her body could respond with any more pleasure, but soon Daisy's breaths grew shorter as Winterbourne pushed into her even harder and more quickly, holding her tightly around her waist with both hands. In a matter of seconds, they shared a convulsing, radiating ecstasy more heavy and luscious than either of them had ever dreamed. Winterbourne kissed her slowly and motioned to run his hands through her hair, but she grabbed his wrist. Her heartbreaking smile curled once again upon her lips. Winterbourne spoke first as Daisy rose herself very matter-of-factly, bent over, and put on her inner skirts. "I must have you again, and forever now as my wife. For I suppose I've claimed you for myself, as it stands, and I would rather die of the Roman fever than to have it any other way."

Daisy let her eyes fall, "It was the best time I've ever had with a gentleman, and I will take that into account. But a lady such as myself should be able to decide her own betrothal with complete certainty," she said in a way that Winterbourne thought oddly detached, but warm nevertheless.

"I must say, I thought a lady of your status, or any status rather, would not kiss me so passionately, and take my very heart into her hands, had she not meant to marry me in earnest."

They sat in glum silence as Daisy picked up her red-ribboned slippers, the color the only thing about her that hinted at her inner sexual desires. "We are both fools, then," finally replied Daisy, "I mustn't linger. This party is bad as it is, and you made a fool of me even more so, now."

Daisy smoothed her hair and dashed out after shutting the light. Winterbourne, confused, hastened after her abrupt departure to catch up with her at the back entrance to the room of the party. "Don't be angry," he whispered hoarsely when she had made her way to some dark corner of the party. "Both your vivaciousness and your beauty deserve more care than you running off to another man after our sublime fuck." Daisy then spotted Giovanelli, laughing with a guest. He smiled back at Daisy, and she turned once more to the dejected Winterbourne.

"I prefer weak tea!" cried Daisy, and she went off with the brilliant Giovanelli. She sat with him in the adjoining room, in the embrasure of the window, for the rest of the evening. There was an interesting performance at the piano, but neither of these young people gave heed to it. When Daisy came to take leave of Mrs. Walker, this lady conscientiously repaired the weakness of which she had been guilty at the moment of the young girl's arrival. She turned her back straight upon Miss Miller and left her to depart with what grace she might. Winterbourne was standing near the door; he saw it all. Daisy turned very pale and looked at her mother, but Mrs. Miller was humbly unconscious of any violation of the usual social forms. She appeared, indeed, to have felt an incongruous impulse to draw attention to her own striking observance of them. "Good night, Mrs. Walker," she said; "we've had a beautiful evening. You see, if I let Daisy come to parties without me, I don't want her to go away without me." Daisy turned away, looking with a pale, grave face at the circle near the door; Winterbourne saw that, for the first moment, she was too much shocked and puzzled even for indignation. He on his side was greatly touched.

"That was very cruel," he said to Mrs. Walker.

"She never enters my drawing room again!" replied his hostess.

Since Winterbourne was not to meet her in Mrs. Walker's drawing room, he went as often as possible to Mrs. Miller's hotel. The ladies were rarely at home, but when he found them, the devoted Giovanelli was always present. Very often the brilliant little Roman was in the drawing room with Daisy alone, Mrs. Miller being apparently constantly of the opinion that discretion is the better part of surveillance. Winterbourne noted, at first with surprise, that Daisy on these occasions was never embarrassed or annoyed by his own entrance; but he very presently began to feel that she had no more surprises for him; the unexpected in her behavior was the only thing to expect.

She showed no displeasure at her tete-a-tete with Giovanelli being interrupted; she could chatter as freshly and freely with two gentlemen as with one; there was always, in her conversation, the same odd mixture of audacity and puerility. Winterbourne remarked to himself that if she was seriously interested in Giovanelli, it was very singular that she should not take more trouble to preserve the sanctity of their interviews; and he liked her the more for her innocent-looking indifference and her apparently inexhaustible good humor. He could hardly have said why, but she seemed to him a girl who would never be jealous.

At the risk of exciting a somewhat derisive smile on the reader's part, I may affirm that with regard to the women who had hitherto interested him, it very often seemed to Winterbourne among the possibilities that, given certain contingencies, he should be afraid—literally afraid—of these ladies; he had a pleasant sense that he should never be afraid of Daisy Miller. It must be added that this sentiment was not altogether flattering to Daisy; it was part of his conviction, or rather of his apprehension, that she would prove a very light young person.

But she was evidently very much interested in Giovanelli. She looked at him whenever he spoke; she was perpetually telling him to do this and to do that; she was constantly "chaffing" and abusing him. She appeared completely to have forgotten that Winterbourne had said anything to displease her at Mrs. Walker's little party. One Sunday afternoon, having gone to St. Peter's with his aunt, Winterbourne perceived Daisy strolling about the great church in company with the inevitable Giovanelli. Presently he pointed out the young girl and her cavalier to Mrs. Costello. This lady looked at them a moment through her eyeglass, and then she said:

"That's what makes you so pensive in these days, eh?"

"I had not the least idea I was pensive," said the young man.

"You are very much preoccupied; you are thinking of something."

"And what is it," he asked, "that you accuse me of thinking of?"

"Of that young lady's—Miss Baker's, Miss Chandler's—what's her name?—Miss Miller's intrigue with that little barber's block."

"Do you call it an intrigue," Winterbourne asked—"an affair that goes on with such peculiar publicity?"

"That's their folly," said Mrs. Costello; "it's not their merit."

"No," rejoined Winterbourne, with something of that pensiveness to which his aunt had alluded. "I don't believe that there is anything to be called an intrigue."

"I have heard a dozen people speak of it; they say she is quite carried away by him."

"They are certainly very intimate," said Winterbourne.

Mrs. Costello inspected the young couple again with her optical instrument. "He is very handsome. One easily sees how it is. She thinks him the most elegant man in the world, the finest gentleman. She has never seen anything like him; he is better, even, than the courier. It was the courier probably who introduced him; and if he succeeds in marrying the young lady, the courier will come in for a magnificent commission."

"I don't believe she thinks of marrying him," said Winterbourne, "and I don't believe he hopes to marry her."

"You may be very sure she thinks of nothing. She goes on from day to day, from hour to hour, as they did in the Golden Age. I can imagine nothing more vulgar. And at the same time," added Mrs. Costello, "depend upon it that she may tell you any moment that she is 'engaged.'"

"I think that is more than Giovanelli expects," said Winterbourne.

"Who is Giovanelli?"

"The little Italian. I have asked questions about him and learned something. He is apparently a perfectly respectable little man. I believe he is, in a small way, a cavaliere avvocato. But he doesn't move in what are called the first circles. I think it is really not absolutely impossible that the courier introduced him. He is evidently immensely charmed with Miss Miller. If she thinks him the finest gentleman in the world, he, on his side, has never found himself in personal contact with such splendor, such opulence, such expensiveness as this young lady's. And then she must seem to him wonderfully pretty and interesting. I rather doubt that he dreams of marrying her. That must appear to him too impossible a piece of luck. He has nothing but his handsome face to offer, and there is a substantial Mr. Miller in that mysterious land of dollars. Giovanelli knows that he hasn't a title to offer. If he were only a count or a marchese! He must wonder at his luck, at the way they have taken him up."

"He accounts for it by his handsome face and thinks Miss Miller a young lady qui se passe ses fantaisies!" said Mrs. Costello.

"It is very true," Winterbourne pursued, "that Daisy and her mamma have not yet risen to that stage of—what shall I call it?—of culture at which the idea of catching a count or a marchese begins. I believe that they are intellectually incapable of that conception."

"Ah! but the avvocato can't believe it," said Mrs. Costello.

Of the observation excited by Daisy's "intrigue," Winterbourne gathered that day at St. Peter's sufficient evidence. A dozen of the

American colonists in Rome came to talk with Mrs. Costello, who sat on a little portable stool at the base of one of the great pilasters. The vesper service was going forward in splendid chants and organ tones in the adjacent choir, and meanwhile, between Mrs. Costello and her friends, there was a great deal said about poor little Miss Miller's going really "too far." Winterbourne was not pleased with what he heard, but when, coming out upon the great steps of the church, he saw Daisy, who had emerged before him, get into an open cab with her accomplice and roll away through the cynical streets of Rome, he could not deny to himself that she was going very far indeed. He felt very sorry for her—not exactly that he believed that she had completely lost her head, but because it was painful to hear so much that was pretty, and undefended, and natural assigned to a vulgar place among the categories of disorder. He made an attempt after this to give a hint to Mrs. Miller. He met one day in the Corso a friend, a tourist like himself, who had just come out of the Doria Palace, where he had been walking through the beautiful gallery. His friend talked for a moment about the superb portrait of Innocent X by Velasquez which hangs in one of the cabinets of the palace, and then said, "And in the same cabinet, by the way, I had the pleasure of contemplating a picture of a different kind—that pretty American girl whom you pointed out to me last week." In answer to Winterbourne's inquiries, his friend narrated that the pretty American girl—prettier than ever—was seated with a companion in the secluded nook in which the great papal portrait was enshrined.

"Who was her companion?" asked Winterbourne.

"A little Italian with a bouquet in his buttonhole. The girl is delightfully pretty, but I thought I understood from you the other day that she was a young lady du meilleur monde."

"So she is!" answered Winterbourne; and having assured himself that his informant had seen Daisy and her companion but five minutes before, he jumped into a cab and went to call on Mrs. Miller. She was at home; but she apologized to him for receiving him in Daisy's absence.

"She's gone out somewhere with Mr. Giovanelli," said Mrs. Miller. "She's always going round with Mr. Giovanelli."

"I have noticed that they are very intimate," Winterbourne observed.

"Oh, it seems as if they couldn't live without each other!" said Mrs. Miller. "Well, he's a real gentleman, anyhow. I keep telling Daisy she's engaged!"

"And what does Daisy say?"

"Oh, she says she isn't engaged. But she might as well be!" this impartial parent resumed; "she goes on as if she was. But I've made Mr. Giovanelli promise to tell me, if *she* doesn't. I should want to write to Mr. Miller about it—shouldn't you?"

Winterbourne replied that he certainly should; and the state of mind of Daisy's mamma struck him as so unprecedented in the annals of parental vigilance that he gave up as utterly irrelevant the attempt to place her upon her guard.

After this Daisy was never at home, and Winterbourne ceased to meet her at the houses of their common acquaintances, because, as he perceived, these shrewd people had quite made up their minds that she was going too far. They ceased to invite her; and they intimated that they desired to express to observant Europeans the great truth that, though Miss Daisy Miller was a young American lady, her behavior was not representative— was regarded by her compatriots as abnormal. Winterbourne wondered how she felt about all the cold shoulders that were turned toward her, and sometimes it annoyed him to suspect that she did not feel at all. He said to himself that she was too light and childish, too uncultivated and unreasoning, too provincial, to have reflected upon her ostracism, or even to have perceived it. Then at other moments he believed that she carried about in her elegant and irresponsible little organism a defiant, passionate, perfectly observant consciousness of the impression she produced.

He asked himself whether Daisy's defiance came from the consciousness of innocence, or from her being, essentially, a young person of the reckless class. It must be admitted that holding one's self to a belief in Daisy's "innocence" came to seem to Winterbourne more and more a matter of fine-spun gallantry. As I have already had occasion to relate, he was angry at finding himself reduced to chopping logic about this young lady; he was vexed at his want of instinctive certitude as to how far her eccentricities were generic, national, and how far they were personal. From either view of them he had somehow missed her, and now it was too late. She was "carried away" by Mr. Giovanelli.

A few days after his brief interview with her mother, he encountered her in that beautiful abode of flowering desolation known as the Palace of the Caesars. The early Roman spring had filled the air with bloom and perfume, and the rugged surface of the Palatine was muffled with tender verdure. Daisy was strolling along the top of one of those great mounds of ruin that are embanked with mossy marble and paved with monumental inscriptions. It seemed to him that Rome had never been so lovely as just then. He stood, looking off at the enchanting harmony of line and color that remotely encircles the city, inhaling the softly humid odors, and feeling the freshness of the year and the antiquity of the place reaffirm themselves in mysterious interfusion. It seemed to him also that Daisy had never looked so pretty, but this had been an observation of his whenever he met her. Giovanelli was at her side, and Giovanelli, too, wore an aspect of even unwonted brilliancy.

"Well," said Daisy, "I should think you would be lonesome!"

"Lonesome?" asked Winterbourne.

"You are always going round by yourself. Can't you get anyone to walk with you?"

"I am not so fortunate," said Winterbourne, "as your companion."

Giovanelli, from the first, had treated Winterbourne with distinguished politeness. He listened with a deferential air to his remarks; he laughed punctiliously at his pleasantries; he seemed disposed to testify to his belief that Winterbourne was a superior young man. He carried himself in no degree like a jealous wooer; he had obviously a great deal of tact; he had no objection to your expecting a little humility of him. It even seemed to Winterbourne at times that Giovanelli would find a certain mental relief in being able to have a private understanding with him—to say to him, as an intelligent man, that, bless you, *he* knew how extraordinary was this young lady, and didn't flatter himself with delusive—or at least *too* delusive—hopes of matrimony and dollars. On this occasion he strolled away from his companion to pluck a sprig of almond blossom, which he carefully arranged in his buttonhole.

"I know why you say that," said Daisy, watching Giovanelli. "Because you think I go round too much with *him*." And she nodded at her attendant.

"Every one thinks so—if you care to know," said Winterbourne.

"Of course I care to know!" Daisy exclaimed seriously. "But I don't believe it. They are only pretending to be shocked. They don't really care a straw what I do. Besides, I don't go round so much."

"I think you will find they do care. They will show it disagreeably."

Daisy looked at him a moment. "How disagreeably?"

"Haven't you noticed anything?" Winterbourne asked.

"I have noticed you. But I noticed you were as stiff as an umbrella the first time I saw you."

"You will find I am not so stiff as several others," said Winterbourne, smiling.

"How shall I find it?"

"By going to see the others."

"What will they do to me?"

"They will give you the cold shoulder. Do you know what that means?"

Daisy was looking at him intently; she began to color. "Do you mean as Mrs. Walker did the other night?"

"Exactly!" said Winterbourne.

She looked away at Giovanelli, who was decorating himself with his almond blossom. Then looking back at Winterbourne, "I shouldn't think you would let people be so unkind!" she said.

"How can I help it?" he asked.

"I should think you would say something."

"I do say something;" and he paused a moment. "I say that your mother tells me that she believes you are engaged."

"Well, she does," said Daisy very simply.

Winterbourne began to laugh. "And does Randolph believe it?" he asked.

"I guess Randolph doesn't believe anything," said Daisy. Randolph's skepticism excited Winterbourne to further hilarity, and he observed that Giovanelli was coming back to them. Daisy, observing it too, addressed herself again to her countryman. "Since you have mentioned it," she said, "I AM engaged." Winterbourne looked at her; he had stopped laughing. "You don't believe!" she added.

He was silent a moment; and then, "Yes, I believe it," he said.

"Oh, no, you don't!" she answered. "Well, then—I am not!"

The young girl and her cicerone were on their way to the gate of the enclosure, so that Winterbourne, who had but lately entered, presently took leave of them. A week afterward he went to dine at a beautiful villa on the Caelian Hill, and, on arriving, dismissed his hired vehicle. The evening was charming, and he promised himself the satisfaction of walking home beneath the Arch of Constantine and past the vaguely lighted monuments of the Forum. There was a waning moon in the sky, and her radiance was not brilliant, but she was veiled in a thin cloud curtain which seemed to diffuse and equalize it. When, on his return from the villa (it was eleven o'clock), Winterbourne approached the dusky circle of the Colosseum, it recurred to him, as a lover of the picturesque, that the interior, in the pale moonshine, would be well worth a glance. He turned aside and walked to one of the empty arches, near which, as he observed, an open carriage—one of the little Roman streetcabs—was stationed. Then he passed in, among the cavernous shadows of the great structure, and emerged upon the clear and silent arena.

The place had never seemed to him more impressive. One-half of the gigantic circus was in deep shade, the other was sleeping in the luminous dusk. As he stood there he began to murmur Byron's famous lines, out of "Manfred," but before he had finished his quotation he remembered that if nocturnal meditations in the Colosseum are recommended by the poets, they are deprecated by the doctors. The historic atmosphere was there, certainly; but the historic atmosphere, scientifically considered, was no better than a villainous miasma. Winterbourne walked to the middle of the arena, to take a more general glance, intending thereafter to make a hasty retreat. The great cross in the center was covered with shadow; it was only as he drew near it that he made it out distinctly. Then he saw that two persons were stationed upon the low steps which formed its base. One of these was a woman, seated; her companion was standing in front of her.

Presently the sound of the woman's voice came to him distinctly in the warm night air. "Well, he looks at us as one of the old lions or tigers may have looked at the Christian martyrs!" These were the words he heard, in the familiar accent of Miss Daisy Miller.

"Let us hope he is not very hungry," responded the ingenious Giovanelli. "He will have to take me first; you will serve for dessert!"

Winterbourne stopped, with a sort of horror, and, it must be added, with a sort of relief. It was as if a sudden illumination had been flashed upon the ambiguity of Daisy's behavior, and the riddle had become easy to read. She was a young lady whom a gentleman need no longer be at pains to respect. He stood there, looking at her—looking at her companion and not reflecting that though he saw them vaguely, he himself must have been more brightly visible. He felt angry with himself that he had bothered so much about the right way of regarding Miss Daisy Miller. Then, as he was going to advance again, he checked himself, not from the fear that he was doing her injustice, but from a sense of the danger of appearing unbecomingly exhilarated by this sudden revulsion from cautious criticism. He turned away toward the entrance of the place, but, as he did so, he heard Daisy speak again.

"Why, it was Mr. Winterbourne! He saw me, and he cuts me!"

What a clever little reprobate she was, and how smartly she played at injured innocence! But he wouldn't cut her. Winterbourne came forward again and went toward the great cross. Daisy had got up; Giovanelli lifted his hat. Winterbourne had now begun to think simply of the craziness, from a sanitary point of view, of a delicate young girl lounging away the evening in this nest of malaria. What if she WERE a clever little reprobate? that was no reason for her dying of the perniciosa. "How long have you been here?" he asked almost brutally.

Daisy, lovely in the flattering moonlight, looked at him a moment. Then—"All the evening," she answered, gently. I never saw anything so pretty."

"I am afraid," said Winterbourne, "that you will not think Roman fever very pretty. This is the way people catch it. I wonder," he added, turning to Giovanelli, "that you, a native Roman, should countenance such a terrible indiscretion."

"Ah," said the handsome native, "for myself I am not afraid."

"Neither am I—for you! I am speaking for this young lady."

Giovanelli lifted his well-shaped eyebrows and showed his brilliant teeth. But he took Winterbourne's rebuke with docility. "I told the signorina it was a grave indiscretion, but when was the signorina ever prudent?"

"I never was sick, and I don't mean to be!" the signorina declared. "I don't look like much, but I'm healthy! I was bound to see the Colosseum by moonlight; I shouldn't have wanted to go home without that; and we have had the most beautiful time, haven't we, Mr. Giovanelli? If there has been any danger, Eugenio can give me some pills. He has got some splendid pills."

"I should advise you," said Winterbourne, "to drive home as fast as possible and take one!"

"What you say is very wise," Giovanelli rejoined. "I will go and make sure the carriage is at hand." And he went forward rapidly.

Daisy followed with Winterbourne. He kept looking at her; she seemed not in the least embarrassed. Winterbourne said nothing; Daisy chattered about the beauty of the place. "Well, I *have* seen the Colosseum by moonlight!" she exclaimed. "That's one good thing." Then, noticing Winterbourne's silence, she asked him why he didn't speak. He made no answer; he only began to laugh. They passed under one of the dark archways; Giovanelli was in front with the carriage. Here Daisy stopped a moment, looking at the young American. "*Did* you believe I was engaged, the other day?" she asked.

"It doesn't matter what I believed the other day," said Winterbourne, still laughing.

"Well, what do you believe now?"

"I believe that it makes very little difference whether you are engaged or not!"

He felt the young girl's pretty eyes fixed upon him through the thick gloom of the archway; she was apparently going to answer. But Giovanelli hurried her forward. "Quick! Quick!" he said; "if we get in by midnight we are quite safe."

Daisy took her seat in the carriage, and the fortunate Italian placed himself beside her. "Don't forget Eugenio's pills!" said Winterbourne as he lifted his hat.

"I don't care," said Daisy in a little strange tone, "whether I have Roman fever or not!" Upon this the cab driver cracked his whip, and they rolled away over the desultory patches of the antique pavement.

Winterbourne, to do him justice, as it were, mentioned to no one that he had encountered Miss Miller, at midnight, in the Colosseum with a gentleman; but nevertheless, a couple of days later, the fact of her having been there under these circumstances was known to every member of the little American circle, and commented accordingly. Winterbourne reflected that they had of course known it at the hotel, and that, after Daisy's return, there had been an exchange of remarks between the porter and the cab driver. But the young man was conscious, at the same moment, that it had ceased to be a matter of serious regret to him that the little American flirt should be "talked about" by low-minded menials. These people, a day or two later, had serious information to give: the little American flirt was alarmingly ill. Winterbourne, when the rumor came to him, immediately went to the hotel for more news. He found that two or three charitable friends had preceded him, and that they were being entertained in Mrs. Miller's salon by Randolph.

"It's going round at night," said Randolph—"that's what made her sick. She's always going round at night. I shouldn't think she'd want to, it's so plaguy dark. You can't see anything here at night, except when there's a moon. In America there's always a moon!" Mrs. Miller was invisible; she was now, at least, giving her daughter the advantage of her society. It was evident that Daisy was dangerously ill.

Winterbourne went often to ask for news of her, and once he saw Mrs. Miller, who, though deeply alarmed, was, rather to his surprise, perfectly composed, and, as it appeared, a most efficient and judicious nurse. She talked a good deal about Dr. Davis, but Winterbourne paid her the compliment of saying to himself that she was not, after all, such a monstrous goose. "Daisy spoke of you the other day," she said to him. "Half the time she doesn't know what she's saying, but that time I think she did. She gave me a message she told me to tell you. She told me to tell you that she never was engaged to that handsome Italian. I am sure I am very glad; Mr. Giovanelli hasn't been near us since she was taken ill. I thought he was so much of a gentleman; but I don't call that very polite! A lady told me that he was afraid I was angry with him for taking Daisy round at night. Well, so I am, but I suppose he knows I'm a lady. I would scorn to scold him. Anyway, she says she's not engaged. I don't know why she wanted you to know, but she said to me three times, 'Mind you tell Mr. Winterbourne.' And then she told me to ask if you remembered the time you went to that castle in Switzerland. But I said I wouldn't give any such messages as that. Only, if she is not engaged, I'm sure I'm glad to know it."

But, as Winterbourne had said, it mattered very little. Daisy had imparted herself to a mere situation of arousal and failure. Oh, if it were true that the following happened, Winterbourne might have been so forlorn as to swear off studying whatsoever. He promptly returned home, pulled up the covers on the chaise unused since last winter, and slept soundly, dipping into a reverie.

He immediately dreamt that a week after this, the poor girl died; it had been a terrible case of the fever. Daisy's grave was in the little Protestant cemetery, in an angle of the wall of imperial Rome, beneath the cypresses and the thick spring flowers. Winterbourne stood there beside it, with a number of other mourners, a number larger than the scandal excited by the young lady's career would have led you to expect. Near him stood Giovanelli, who came nearer still before Winterbourne turned away. Giovanelli was very pale: on this occasion he had no flower in his buttonhole; he seemed to wish to say something. At last he said, "She was the most beautiful young lady I ever saw, and the most amiable;" and then he added in a moment, "and she was the most innocent."

Winterbourne looked at him and presently repeated his words, "And the most innocent?"

"The most innocent!"

Winterbourne felt sore and angry. "Why the devil," he asked, "did you take her to that fatal place?"

Mr. Giovanelli's urbanity was apparently imperturbable. He looked on the ground a moment, and then he said, "For myself I had no fear; and she wanted to go."

"That was no reason!" Winterbourne declared.

The subtle Roman again dropped his eyes. "If she had lived, I should have got nothing. She would never have married me, I am sure."

"She would never have married you?"

"For a moment I hoped so. But no. I am sure."

Winterbourne listened to him: he stood staring at the raw protuberance among the April daisies. When he turned away again, Mr. Giovanelli, with his light, slow step, had retired.

Winterbourne almost immediately left Rome; but the following summer he again met his aunt, Mrs. Costello at Vevey. Mrs. Costello was fond of Vevey. In the interval Winterbourne had often thought of Daisy Miller and her mystifying manners. One day he spoke of her to his aunt—said it was on his conscience that he had done her injustice.

"I am sure I don't know," said Mrs. Costello. "How did your injustice affect her?"

"She sent me a message before her death which I didn't understand at the time; but I have understood it since. She would have appreciated one's esteem."

"Is that a modest way," asked Mrs. Costello, "of saying that she would have reciprocated one's affection?"

Frederick Winterbourne awoke with every muscle aching sorely, next to the edge of the chaise, on the floor. He looked to his bare left leg; a bruise had appeared after his falling rudely in the very middle of the night, and the soreness had begun to reverberate and shatter through his rêve fantasmagorique. The dialogue of the dream had a gargled, groggy way about it, and Winterbourne lay on his back for a few minutes debating his options. He had felt utterly subdued by Daisy's inpenetrable nature on several occasions. To him, in these past few days after Miss Walker's party, Daisy was a calculus on his happiness, invading his independent thoughts like a fresh vine on a trellis. To say the very least, she was beginning to unnerve him in a way that was foreign and uncomfortable. He could shoot himself. After all, *she* would never allow him the coup de grace. Her sweet smile had played him for a fool when she wasn't even in the same city. Unless he was mistaken, she had even said this at Miss Walker's party. Yet he was a haunted man. Should he forever abandon his desire for her hand, her brilliant and soft tongue, her tears of sadness and happy moments?

Winterbourne offered no answer to this question remaining from his dream; but he presently said to himself, "Miss Costello was right in that remark she made last summer. I was booked to make a mistake. I have lived too long in foreign parts."

He sat on the nearest chair, brooding for hours. All of this was spot on. He had practically thrown himself in her way until he exhausted himself, and he was not known for such behavior. Daisy, for all practical purposes, had turned him into a gentleman-at-arms. He felt that he must at all costs not give up on her cause. It would be worse than the Roman fever for *him*. From whence he slept, he decided once and for all he would stop this silliness and bid her confess herself, or board the new Cunard on the way to somewhere, *anywhere*, shortly after.

Winterbourne massaged his temples, groaning at the thought of confronting the petite, sick girl. When he arrived to Daisy's apartment, he cast his eyes to the ceiling, appreciating fully the lack of Mr. Giovanelli. He was received immediately by Mrs. Miller. "Mr. Winterbourne! I willed you to come over the night Daisy came down with this terrible illness, but Daisy forebade me from inviting even Randolph to play at her bedside. Even his pleasant follies have disturbed her, pained though she is to admit it."

Winterbourne nodded and blushed. He thought to himself he must appear a souse, hair disheveled and silent. He murmured a hello and inquired politely about the affairs of Mrs. Miller's health as well as the fragile state of her daughter. Mrs. Miller replied bluntly. "My dear, you have visited her so often since she was taken sick that you must care a great deal about her health. I implore you to make this clear to Daisy, as young ladies of our family's standing can be as unwavering as bulls in their callousness toward suitors of yours. Perhaps putting it delicately will help your cause. It could be the reason for her lingering sickness, one might say."

Winterbourne stepped back involuntarily when these fiery words were uttered. Was his infatuation so obvious that even Daisy's mother tired of his presence? And what did Mrs. Miller mean by "it could be the reason for her lingering sickness"? it crossed his mind that Mrs. Miller may be more manipulative than he bargained for. It must make *her* violently ill to see her daughter cavort with the underclass, after all! Though barely sated with her daughter's rejection of Giovanelli as a husband, Mrs. Miller probably would pay Winterbourne a dowry three times whatever Giovanelli would accept, just to avoid Daisy dipping herself lower into social displays.

Winterbourne saw that Mrs. Miller's smile had hardened again; he interjected before she could say another word. "Mrs. Miller, if she will take me, I will spirit your daughter away from the people you have been acquainted with here in Rome. I have arranged for the sale of Chillon as an historical property. It is still the property of Switzerland, Vevey, of course, but I've come across a considerable amount of political clout, courtesy of my newly minted lawyer friends.

The private upper rampart area, with its twenty-one rooms, well I should hope Daisy would visit me there. All of the Millers are more than welcome.

At this, Mrs. Miller's hand clutched at her heart in a violent manner, and Winterbourne wondered for a flickering moment how he'd best run to her aid. Would she need smelling salts, or water? But then Mrs. Miller applied a beige silk handkerchief to her nose and spoke softly. "Daisy has been crying out for you in the middle of the night. Her trip to Chillon hangs heavy in her mind, and she wishes for nothing more than to speak with you." Mrs. Miller's sleeve was in tatters. To the point that her dressing gown looked as though it could be torn by one mistakenly shoving one's arm through the moth-eaten holes in the side a number of times, before finally getting it through the sleeve.

The funneling of the fiduciary means of the family into Daisy's care showed in small ways such as these. With that, Winterbourne gained some resolve. "Please grant me the opportunity to entertain Daisy with my presence, if nothing else. I will be gentle as a lamb, I swear it." Not another word passed between them as Mrs. Miller led him to Daisy's bedside and abruptly left to tend to Randolph. Winterbourne didn't waste a moment in kneeling tenderly by Daisy's bedside.

She looked dew-eyed, as if she had been crying only moments before, but straightened up when Winterbourne walked in. "Daisy, I have infinite regrets in how I left you in the care of that, that cur, Giovanelli. The dog should be hung. You are the only girl for me, so please, if you ask of me anything, I should do it without hesitation. Please just accept this small sum, if only as a loan, as I can only hope you'll make a full recovery."

Winterbourne laid a large money sack on her nightstand and grasped Daisy's little hand so tightly, she gave him a tight smile and giggled, covering her mouth with the other, now unnaturally slender arm. She spoke in a taunting yet soft voice.

"Winterbourne, I am nineteen. What are you asking of me? Do you wish to donate a sizeable part of your family's riches to mine simply because you enjoy my company? Or do you—"

"Daisy, I can't pretend I don't love you!" blurted Winterbourne. She turned as red as the turnips in her hometown, and Winterbourne did the same. They sat in silence, Daisy on her elbows in her bed. Then —

"Winterbourne, I thought you were simply going to ask if you'd wanted us to pay you back with interest after my father sends the money. I assume courtship isn't a condition of this lending. But very well, I will sell off my filigreed dresses from when I am well until the Millers have paid their debt to you. I can't go about dying, and the medicine isn't so costly anyway." She looked at him as a lioness might look after experiencing an injury at the hooves of her prey. "And Winterbourne, as for the question of courtship, my answer is that it should be a splendid competition. Between you and so many of my other 'suitors' as the other Americans are fond of saying. Consider yourself in the running. But whether you end up champion or vice champion of my heart, I will decide. *All* wagers are *off*. I tire of this flirtatiousness, and in fact wish to be betrothed in a matter of a week. You have been frank with me, so I will be frank with you, Winterbourne. I don't think there's anything wrong with flirting, and if I am to be betrothed, why should I hesitate to have a little, shall we say, fun?"

"But Daisy! What do you mean?" Winterbourne gasped out.

"Winterbourne, you are very close to the finish line, to my heart. I know you are a generous, caring, winsome man, and you are very dear to me. But there are so many others in kind who would jump up at the opportunity to woo me. I want the chance to explore my options, at least between you and dear Giovanelli, who have also shown me many kindnesses. Neither of you has fought for me in the way I wish to be fought for, and perhaps that is why you two have made it this far in competition for my heart. I only propose continuing the competition."

Winterbourne thought about this. If he had a fifty-per-cent chance of marrying his beloved Daisy, he had a one-hundred-per-cent chance of being lovesick to the end of his days if he didn't even try. He imagined the mention of Giovanelli's name might be a distraction from her hesitance at being so young. He told Daisy he was up for the challenge, and leaned in. He put his hand behind her fair cheek. He sat softly next to her. He kissed her deeply and passionately, and she trembled, melting into their shared, sacred moment.

Then she opened her eyes. A great tear rolled down her cheek. "Of—Of course, you and Giovanelli are free to pursue other—more traditional—ladies as well."

For an ill violet, Daisy was as pretty as ever. Winterbourne ordered her to hush. "Daisy, you are not a negotiator at heart. I've already said that you're the one for me. But if you dare, test my love and dedication in the next week, and I shall surely prove myself." Daisy nodded in her bright, delicate way. Winterbourne bent down to give her a kiss goodbye, and she rolled her eyes and gave him a naughty, slight smile.

"I feel better already," she said.

Winterbourne left, puzzled. He'd never felt more perplexed, and he'd never felt more alive. He was perspiring, and went to bed immediately.

He woke up famished and set himself to work. He did not think of Giovanelli, and he certainly did not think of Daisy. He received reports from time to time from mutual friends about her full recovery, and about her excursions into Florence with Giovanelli and others, but he never heard of an intimate moment. After four days though, he began to think that Daisy's affections might have been, in fact, bestowed upon several men as she insisted, as she did not call on him. He thought of moving to America, and of forgetting her forever. He visited a few expatriate friends and made the most of her absence, forcing himself to think of continuing the charade of a full life without her; after all, barring their conversation as she was ill, her abandonment was all but complete since Miss Walker's party.

On the sixth day, Winterbourne made an effort of gathering his things into his many valises and even his two portmanteaux in an effort to rid himself of the accumulating gloom surrounding the prospects of her return, in an effort to leave Rome for the comfort of old friends in Switzerland.

• • •

Winterbourne finished placing his belongings, pulled his sheet-tops out, prepared his traveler's suit, and went to bed, thinking of the next day's journey back to Geneva. Sleep came easily. But not two hours later, a pitter-patter sound awoke him. He thought it was the rainy season approaching, and went to close the shutters in the powder room. But the rain had stopped hours ago, as he could see that the carriages just outside were bone dry.

Seeing a movement outside, he asked who it was at midnight, and what business they had waking him up. A tinny voice answered, and he immediately opened the door, his dressing gown trailing on the wooden floor. Daisy made her way into his apartment without invitation. "I have thought about this, Winterbourne, since we met. And I have had a wonderful time walking in the gardens and through the brilliant palazzos of Rome with Giovanelli. But

I haven't so much as pecked him on the cheek, as is the custom here. Because, Winterbourne, you have my heart."

Winterbourne closed his eyes and breathed in her raindrop-scented hair. He picked her up at once, and carried her into his feather bed. He laid her down, and with unforeseen skill, Winterbourne unfurled her hair and untied her bodice. After embracing each other in the nude for several minutes, Winterbourne whispered. "I knew you were prone to come back into my arms, my dear, from the moment we met."

Daisy, ever the bright little coquette, observed that he didn't. "Then I suppose your portmanteaux ambled by themselves to the door?"

Winterbourne had had enough. He grabbed her waist and squeezed until Daisy made a rather unpleasant face, but this pleased him even more, as he knew she desired him. Daisy drew his hands down into her downy hairs above her sex, and smiled. Winterbourne knelt, grabbed her near, drew her onto his finger, and slowly made his finger's way into her. He then sat on the bed and beckoned her over. She was still smiling, and at once she sat down in Winterbourne's lap, where he immediately started to massage her demure little breasts. She began to rub herself up and down his body, and soon they could help themselves no longer: Ravenous for love, they pushed into each other, and Winterbourne shoved his prick into Daisy's peach until they both felt an immediate sensation of blinding pleasure.

Daisy Miller and Frederick Winterbourne carried on like alley cats in the night, and the very next day traveled hand-in-hand to Florence, where on the Ponte Vecchio they presented each other with hammered gold rings, much to the bemusement of the watching countrymen. Of course, by that time, Winterbourne had given instructions to the town of Vevey to retain the property of the castle at Chillon. Daisy only shrugged at this news. Winterbourne didn't mind—nevertheless, they went back to live at Geneva for the rest of their lives intertwined, whence there continue to come the most contradictory accounts of his motives of sojourn: a report that he is "studying" hard—an intimation that he is much still interested in a very clever foreign lady.

A Sneak Peek from Crimson Romance
(From *The Count of Monte Cristo: The Wild and Wanton Edition, Vol 1* by Monica Corwin and Alexandre Dumas)

On the 24th of February, 1815, the look-out at Notre-Dame de la Garde signaled the three-master, the *Pharaon* from Smyrna, Trieste, and Naples.

As usual, a pilot put off immediately, and rounding the Chateau d'If, got on board the vessel between Cape Morgion and Rion Island.

Immediately, and according to custom, the ramparts of Fort Saint-Jean were covered with spectators; it is always an event at Marseilles for a ship to come into port, especially when this ship, like the *Pharaon*, has been built, rigged, and laden at the old Phocee docks, and belongs to an owner of the city.

The ship drew on and had safely passed the strait and approached the harbor under topsails, jib, and spanker, but so slowly and sedately that the idlers, with that instinct which is the forerunner of evil, asked one another what misfortune could have happened on board. However, those experienced in navigation saw plainly that if any accident had occurred, it was not to the vessel herself, for the pilot, who was steering the *Pharaon* towards the narrow entrance of the inner port, was a young man, who, with activity and vigilant eye, watched every motion of the ship, and repeated each direction of the pilot.

The vague disquietude which prevailed among the spectators had so much affected one of the crowd that he did not await the arrival of the vessel in harbor, but jumping into a small skiff, desired to be pulled alongside the *Pharaon*, which he reached as she rounded into La Reserve basin.

When the young man on board saw this person approach, he left his station by the pilot, and, hat in hand, leaned over the ship's bulwarks.

He was a fine, tall, slim young fellow of eighteen or twenty, with black eyes, and hair as dark as a raven's wing; and his whole appearance bespoke that calmness and resolution peculiar to men accustomed from their cradle to contend with danger.

"Ah, is it you, Dantes?" cried the man in the skiff. "What's the matter? And why have you such an air of sadness aboard?"

"A great misfortune, M. Morrel," replied the young man,—"a great misfortune, for me especially! Off Civita Vecchia we lost our brave Captain Leclere."

"And the cargo?" inquired the owner, eagerly.

"Is all safe, M. Morrel; and I think you will be satisfied on that head. But poor Captain Leclere—"

"What happened to him?" asked the owner, with an air of considerable resignation. "What happened to the worthy captain?"

"He died."

"Fell into the sea?"

"No, sir, he died of brain-fever in dreadful agony." Then turning to the crew, he said, "Bear a hand there, to take in sail!"

All hands obeyed, and at once the eight or ten seamen who composed the crew, sprang to their respective stations. The young sailor gave a look to see that his orders were promptly and accurately obeyed, and then turned again to the owner.

"And how did this misfortune occur?" inquired the latter, resuming the interrupted conversation.

"Alas, sir, in the most unexpected manner. After a long talk with the harbor-master, Captain Leclere left Naples greatly disturbed in the mind. In twenty-four hours he was attacked by a fever, and died three days afterwards. We performed the usual burial service, and he is at his rest, sewn up in his hammock with a thirty-six pound shot at his head and his heels, off El Giglio

Island. We bring to his widow his sword and cross of honor. It was worthwhile, truly," added the young man with a melancholy smile, "to make war against the English for ten years, and to die in his bed at last, like everybody else."

"Why, you see, Edmond," replied the owner, who appeared more comforted at every moment, "we are all mortal, and the old must make way for the young. If not, why, there would be no promotion; and since you assure me that the cargo—"

"Is all safe and sound, M. Morrel, take my word for it; and I advise you not to take 25,000 francs for the profits of the voyage."

Then, as they were just passing the Round Tower, the young man shouted: "Stand by there to lower the topsails and jib; brail up the spanker!"

The order was executed as promptly as it would have been on board a man-of-war.

"Let go—and clue up!" At this last command all the sails were lowered, and the vessel moved almost imperceptibly onwards.

"Now, if you will come on board, M. Morrel," said Dantes, observing the owner's impatience, "here is your supercargo, M. Danglars, coming out of his cabin, who will furnish you with every particular. As for me, I must look after the anchoring, and dress the ship in mourning."

The owner did not wait for a second invitation. He seized a rope which Dantes flung to him, and with an activity that would have done credit to a sailor, climbed up the side of the ship, while the young man, going to his task, left the conversation to Danglars, who now came towards the owner. He was a man of twenty-five or twenty-six years of age, of unprepossessing countenance, obsequious to his superiors, insolent to his subordinates; and this, in addition to his position as responsible agent on board, which is always obnoxious to the sailors, made him as much disliked by the crew as Edmond Dantes was beloved by them.

"Well, M. Morrel," said Danglars, "you have heard of the misfortune that has befallen us?"

"Yes—yes: poor Captain Leclere! He was a brave and an honest man."

"And a first-rate seaman, one who had seen long and honorable service, as became a man charged with the interests of a house so important as that of Morrel & Son," replied Danglars.

"But," replied the owner, glancing after Dantes, who was watching the anchoring of his vessel, "it seems to me that a sailor need not be so old as you say, Danglars, to understand his business, for our friend Edmond seems to understand it thoroughly, and not to require instruction from any one."

"Yes," said Danglars, darting at Edmond a look gleaming with hate. "Yes, he is young, and youth is invariably self-confident. Scarcely was the captain's breath out of his body when he assumed the command without consulting any one, and he caused us to lose a day and a half at the Island of Elba, instead of making for Marseilles direct."

"As to taking command of the vessel," replied Morrel, "that was his duty as captain's mate; as to losing a day and a half off the Island of Elba, he was wrong, unless the vessel needed repairs."

"The vessel was in as good condition as I am, and as, I hope you are, M. Morrel, and this day and a half was lost from pure whim, for the pleasure of going ashore, and nothing else."

"Dantes," said the ship-owner, turning towards the young man, "come this way!"

"In a moment, sir," answered Dantes, "and I'm with you." Then calling to the crew, he said—"Let go!"

The anchor was instantly dropped, and the chain ran rattling through the port-hole. Dantes continued at his post in spite of the presence of the pilot, until this maneuver was completed, and then he added, "Half-mast the colors, and square the yards!"

"You see," said Danglars, "he fancies himself captain already, upon my word."

"And so, in fact, he is," said the owner.

"Except your signature and your partner's, M. Morrel."

"And why should he not have this?" asked the owner; "he is young, it is true, but he seems to me a thorough seaman, and of full experience."

A cloud passed over Danglars' brow. "Your pardon, M. Morrel," said Dantes, approaching, "the vessel now rides at anchor, and I am at your service. You hailed me, I think?"

Danglars retreated a step or two. "I wished to inquire why you stopped at the Island of Elba?"

"I do not know, sir; it was to fulfill the last instructions of Captain Leclere, who, when dying, gave me a packet for Marshal Bertrand."

"Then did you see him, Edmond?"

"Who?"

"The marshal."

"Yes."

Morrel looked around him, and then, drawing Dantes on one side, he said suddenly—"And how is the emperor?"

"Very well, as far as I could judge from the sight of him."

"You saw the emperor, then?"

"He entered the marshal's apartment while I was there."

"And you spoke to him?"

"Why, it was he who spoke to me, sir," said Dantes, with a smile.

"And what did he say to you?"

"Asked me questions about the vessel, the time she left Marseilles, the course she had taken, and what her cargo was. I believe, if she had not been laden, and I had been her master, he would have bought her. But I told him I was only mate, and that she belonged to the firm of Morrel & Son. 'Ah, yes,' he said, 'I know them. The Morrels have been ship-owners from father to son; and there was a Morrel who served in the same regiment with me when I was in garrison at Valence.'"

"Pardieu, and that is true!" cried the owner, greatly delighted. "And that was Policar Morrel, my uncle, who was afterwards a captain. Dantes, you must tell my uncle that the emperor remembered him, and you will see it will bring tears into the old soldier's eyes. Come, come," continued he, patting Edmond's shoulder kindly, "you did very right, Dantes, to follow Captain Leclere's instructions, and touch at Elba, although if it were known that you had conveyed a packet to the marshal, and had conversed with the emperor, it might bring you into trouble."

"How could that bring me into trouble, sir?" asked Dantes; "for I did not even know of what I was the bearer; and the emperor merely made such inquiries as he would of the first comer. But, pardon me; here are the health officers and the customs inspectors coming alongside." And the young man went to the gangway. As he departed, Danglars approached, and said, —

"Well, it appears that he has given you satisfactory reasons for his landing at Porto-Ferrajo?"

"Yes, most satisfactory, my dear Danglars."

"Well, so much the better," said the supercargo; "for it is not pleasant to think that a comrade has not done his duty."

"Dantes has done his," replied the owner, "and that is not saying much. It was Captain Leclere who gave orders for this delay."

"Talking of Captain Leclere, has not Dantes given you a letter from him?"

"To me?—no—was there one?"

"I believe that, besides the packet, Captain Leclere confided a letter to his care."

"Of what packet are you speaking, Danglars?"

"Why, that which Dantes left at Porto-Ferrajo."

"How do you know he had a packet to leave at Porto-Ferrajo?"

Danglars turned very red.

"I was passing close to the door of the captain's cabin, which was half open, and I saw him give the packet and letter to Dantes."

"He did not speak to me of it," replied the ship-owner; "but if there be any letter he will give it to me."

Danglars reflected for a moment. "Then, M. Morrel, I beg of you," said he, "not to say a word to Dantes on the subject. I may have been mistaken."

At this moment the young man returned; Danglars withdrew.

"Well, my dear Dantes, are you now free?" inquired the owner.

"Yes, sir."

"You have not been long detained."

"No. I gave the custom-house officers a copy of our bill of lading; and as to the other papers, they sent a man off with the pilot, to whom I gave them."

"Then you have nothing more to do here?"

"No—everything is all right now."

"Then you can come and dine with me?"

"I really must ask you to excuse me, M. Morrel. My first visit is due to my father; though I am not the less grateful for the honor you have done me."

"Right, Dantes, quite right. I always knew you were a good son."

"And," inquired Dantes, with some hesitation, "do you know how my father is?"

"Well, I believe, my dear Edmond, though I have not seen him lately."

"Yes, he likes to keep himself shut up in his little room."

"That proves, at least, that he has wanted for nothing during your absence."

Dantes smiled. "My father is proud, sir, and if he had not a meal left, I doubt if he would have asked anything from anyone, except from Heaven."

"Well, then, after this first visit has been made we shall count on you."

"I must again excuse myself, M. Morrel, for after this first visit has been paid I have another which I am most anxious to pay."

"True, Dantes, I forgot that there was at the Catalans someone who expects you no less impatiently than your father—the lovely Mercedes."

Dantes blushed.

"Ah, ha," said the ship-owner, "I am not in the least surprised, for she has been to me three times, inquiring if there were any news of the *Pharaon*. Peste, Edmond, you have a very handsome mistress!"

"She is not my mistress," replied the young sailor, gravely; "she is my betrothed."

"Sometimes one and the same thing," said Morrel, with a smile.

"Not with us, sir," replied Dantes.

"Well, well, my dear Edmond," continued the owner, "don't let me detain you. You have managed my affairs so well that I ought to allow you all the time you require for your own. Do you want any money?"

"No, sir; I have all my pay to take—nearly three months' wages."

"You are a careful fellow, Edmond."

"Say I have a poor father, sir."

"Yes, yes, I know how good a son you are, so now hasten away to see your father. I have a son too, and I should be very wroth with those who detained him from me after a three months' voyage."

"Then I have your leave, sir?"

"Yes, if you have nothing more to say to me."

"Nothing."

"Captain Leclere did not, before he died, give you a letter for me?"

"He was unable to write, sir. But that reminds me that I must ask your leave of absence for some days."

"To get married?"

"Yes, first, and then to go to Paris."

"Very good; have what time you require, Dantes. It will take quite six weeks to unload the cargo, and we cannot get you ready for sea until three months after that; only be back again in three months, for the *Pharaon*," added the owner, patting the young sailor on the back, "cannot sail without her captain."

"Without her captain!" cried Dantes, his eyes sparkling with animation; "pray mind what you say, for you are touching on the most secret wishes of my heart. Is it really your intention to make me captain of the *Pharaon*?"

"If I were sole owner we'd shake hands on it now, my dear Dantes, and call it settled; but I have a partner, and you know the Italian proverb—*Chi ha compagno ha padrone*—'He who has a partner has a master.' But the thing is at least half done, as you have one out of two votes. Rely on me to procure you the other; I will do my best."

"Ah, M. Morrel," exclaimed the young seaman, with tears in his eyes, and grasping the owner's hand, "M. Morrel, I thank you in the name of my father and of Mercedes."

"That's all right, Edmond. There's a providence that watches over the deserving. Go to your father: go and see Mercedes, and afterwards come to me."

"Shall I row you ashore?"

"No, thank you; I shall remain and look over the accounts with Danglars. Have you been satisfied with him this voyage?"

"That is according to the sense you attach to the question, sir. Do you mean is he a good comrade? No, for I think he never liked me since the day when I was silly enough, after a little quarrel we had, to propose to him to stop for ten minutes at the island of Monte Cristo to settle the dispute—a proposition which I was wrong to suggest, and he quite right to refuse. If you mean as responsible agent when you ask me the question, I believe there is nothing to say against him, and that you will be content with the way in which he has performed his duty."

"But tell me, Dantes, if you had command of the *Pharaon* should you be glad to see Danglars remain?"

"Captain or mate, M. Morrel, I shall always have the greatest respect for those who possess the owners' confidence."

"That's right, that's right, Dantes! I see you are a thoroughly good fellow, and will detain you no longer. Go, for I see how impatient you are."

"Then I have leave?"

"Go, I tell you."

"May I have the use of your skiff?"

"Certainly."

"Then, for the present, M. Morrel, farewell, and a thousand thanks!"

"I hope soon to see you again, my dear Edmond. Good luck to you."

The young sailor jumped into the skiff, and sat down in the stern sheets, with the order that he be put ashore at La Canebiere. The two oarsmen bent to their work, and the little boat glided away as rapidly as possible in the midst of the thousand vessels which choke up the narrow way which leads between the two rows of ships from the mouth of the harbor to the Quai d'Orleans.

The ship-owner, smiling, followed him with his eyes until he saw him spring out on the quay and disappear in the midst of the throng, which from five o'clock in the morning until nine o'clock at night, swarms in the famous street of La Canebiere,—a street of which the modern Phocaeans are so proud that they say with all the gravity in the world, and with that accent which gives so much character to what is said, "If Paris had La Canebiere, Paris would be a second Marseilles." On turning round the owner saw

Danglars behind him, apparently awaiting orders, but in reality also watching the young sailor,—but there was a great difference in the expression of the two men who thus followed the movements of Edmond Dantes.

In the mood for more Crimson Romance?
Check out *Far from the Madding Crowd*
by Pan Zador and Thomas Hardy
at *CrimsonRomance.com*.